GW01607146

Richard Jefferies

Under the Acorns

A Selection of Nature Essays

Illustrated and Introduced by
Peter & Carol Cholerton

HORIZON HANDMADE BOOKS

This Volume 1982

Standard Edition ISBN 0 907197 01 9
Limited Edition ISBN 0 907197 02 7

Printed in Great Britain at
The Roundwood Press, Kineton, Warwick

Published by
HORIZON — CHOLERTON
HORIZON HANDMADE BOOKS
35 Luddington Road, Stratford-upon-Avon, Warwickshire
Telephone (0789) 69236

Contents

This Book is Number ...145........
of an Edition Limited to 650 Copies
Hand Bound and Printed Letterpress on
Van Gelder Mould Made Paper

Peter Cholerton.

Introduction

"In the hearts of most of us," wrote Richard Jefferies, "there is always the desire for something beyond experience." The sentence is from his essay *Red Roofs of London*, but the sentiment it contains can be found directly or obliquely in almost everything he wrote. For him the search for "something beyond" was a lifelong quest, an obsession which permeated his thought and his work. His nature essays are a faithful record of what he saw, a world observed both broadly and minutely (epitomised in *The Story of My Heart*, when he sees the sun "lighting the great heaven; gleaming on my finger-nail").

Many others have written — and continue to write — their observations of the countryside. Nature books are a popular genre. What puts Jefferies above so many of the rest is that his writing is suffused with a profound insight into the miracle of all existence. So intense were his feelings that Jefferies claimed his meditations in the countryside often left him physically and mentally exhausted.

But such insight did not satisfy Jefferies. Seeing clearly the fact of the miracle, he sought the key to it; he demanded that which he called "the Beyond." In his autobiography, *The Story of My Heart*, he wrote of his own existence: "I saw its joy, its unhappiness, its birth, its death, its possibilities among the infinite, above all its yearning Question. Why?" And later in the same book: "The fact of my own existence as I write, as I exist at this second, is so marvellous, so miracle-like, strange, and supernatural to me, that I unhesitatingly conclude I am always on the margin of life illimitable, and that there are higher conditions than existence."

The essays and notebooks written towards the end of his life are pervaded with a palpable urgency as Jefferies struggles so desperately to grasp the Beyond (that is, the Whole, a *new idea* to complete man's understanding of Why?). The notebooks make valuable reading for anyone interested in Jefferies' work; the pity is that they are out of print, making them expensive and difficult for the ordinary reader to come by. However they are no place to begin an acquaintanceship with Jefferies, they would be hard going and to a good extent meaningless. Better first to choose from what is readily available, and include *The Story of My Heart* and Edward Thomas's biography *Richard Jefferies*.

It must be said that in contrast to the esoteric notebooks much of Jefferies' writing was at the opposite end of his literary gamut. At one stage of his career almost a score of magazines and periodicals were prepared to accept pieces from him. But, as a professional writer needing to earn his bread and butter, he was obliged to provide that which the editors requested of him, and for the most part that meant nature and rural life essays unadulterated by the search for wider meaning. Such pieces, though pleasant, are often uninspiring and sometimes appear to be little more than the stringing together of observations straight from his field-notes.

This volume is intended as an introduction to Richard Jefferies, and for that reason we have selected essays which in our opinion reveal his insight in its most lucid expression. His personal quest for the unknown is ever present, but it is perfectly controlled and ebbs and flows through the pages carrying the reader on its tides.

But first, a brief life. . . .

Richard Jefferies was born on 6th November 1848, at Coate Farm, in the hamlet of Coate, near Swindon. He was the son of Elizabeth and James Luckett Jefferies.

James Luckett has been described by Edward Thomas as "an original man, an eccentric, a man of character and instincts, . . . and notably clever with his hands." He was born in London in 1816, though the family moved to Swindon within a year of his birth. During his youth he moved a good deal between Wiltshire and London until, at twenty-one, he set sail for North America, probably working his passage. It is not known whether he intended to stay there, but America was certainly a land of opportunity for a fit and enterprising young man, especially one prepared to work the land. It perhaps says something of his character that he preferred to move around working as a farm labourer for a couple of years before returning home. In London he met and courted an Islington girl, Elizabeth Gyde, and married her in 1844. The couple moved directly to Coate Farm, which had been in the Jefferies family since 1800.

Elizabeth was a city girl born and bred and never took easily to the country and the unsocial life she was to lead. James Luckett, being no businessman, became a farmer of little and ever diminishing success, always short of money and sometimes in debt. He was a man given to dreaming more than to practicalities, and the farm's failure was less likely due to misfortune than to lack of endeavour in the right directions. The farm was some forty acres of good soil but James Luckett never troubled to put it to arable use, preferring to make it pasture for dairy cattle to graze. This left him more time to attend to the needs of his first loves, his garden and the planting of trees. He was a known expert on timber both felled and growing, and he went about its cultivation with a rare passion.

In his novel *Amaryllis at the Fair* Richard Jefferies created the characters of Mr and Mrs Iden much in the image of his parents, and evidence of the friction which existed at Coate can be gleaned from the Idens. Mr Iden plants potatoes in a way Jefferies describes as "wonderful, every potato was placed at exactly the right distance apart . . . had he been planting his own children he could not have been more careful. The science, the skill, and the experience brought to this potato-planting you would hardly credit. . . ." But Mrs Iden takes a somewhat different view: "He will never do any good," she says. "Just look at his coat; it's a disgrace, a positive disgrace . . . wasting his time there with potatoes, it is enough to make one wild; why doesn't he go into the market and buy and sell cattle, and turn over money in that way? Not he! He'd rather muddle with a few paltry potatoes, as if it mattered an atom how they were stuck in the ground."

In later years parts of the farm were sold off to meet the bills and, in 1878, the property was sold altogether. In a letter written shortly before his death James Luckett remembers Coate with scant affection. "It was a badly planned house," he said, "with not a room fit to live in. . . . We were all so glad to get away." Of his financial position at the time of leaving he said, "I was not obliged to leave Coate, but I should have been had I stay'd much longer."

James Luckett ended his days working as a gardener in Bath. He outlived his son, Richard, by almost ten years, dying aged 80 in 1896. Elizabeth died the year before.

Richard Jefferies was one of five children. His elder sister was killed by a runaway horse when Richard was only four, and it was at about this time that he was sent away to Sydenham, near London, to live with his aunt and uncle, the Harrilds. Here the boy stayed until he was nine years old, spending only about one month a year at home in Coate. Thomas Harrild was a printer and both Richard's grandfathers had been in the printing and bookbinding trade. The influence of this on Richard was that he became addicted at an early age to reading on a wide range of subjects.

Richard's relationship with his aunt was close and lasting, even in adulthood he claimed to be happier with her than he was at home. Certainly Mrs Harrild was fond of her nephew. She was sympathetic to his aspirations and the atmosphere at Sydenham was more conducive to the needs of his sensitive nature than the crowded cottage in Wiltshire. When he was nineteen he wrote to Mrs Harrild: "I always do feel dull when I leave you, for as I said before I am happier with you than at home, because you enter into my prospects with interest and are always kind."

At school in Swindon he was a good though not brilliant scholar. Reading avidly and retreating regularly to the fields, he was becoming a solitary figure unconsciously educating himself in the manner best suited to his future needs. "He stood aloof from us, never mixing in our games," recalled one fellow pupil. "With head bent forward he always seemed in a study . . . so that it was difficult for anyone to approach him."

Whatever he may have gained from formal schooling it is certain he had a sound knowledge of the classics, Shakespeare, and the Bible. His younger brother, Charles, is reported to have said that Richard's acquaintance with the Bible was very extensive, "and it was difficult for anyone to puzzle him with questions concerning it." Indeed his broad spectrum of religious and philosophical reading makes it difficult to assess precisely to what extent Jefferies was an original thinker; Zoroaster, the Koran, and the Buddhist state of enlightenment, Nirvana, are all mentioned in his writing. But the mature Richard Jefferies was to sweep aside these and all other systems of religion, dismissing them as irrelevant to solving the mystery of ultimate truth, the Beyond. "When I ask myself in the dawn what I know, the answer is nothing. . . . We really *know* no more than the rooks cawking together cawk, cawk, caw in their trees at sunset. They know not where the sun goes; they cawk, they caw, so do the philosophers and prophets." In *The Story of My Heart* he states: "First we must lay down the axiom that as yet nothing has been found; we have nothing to start with; all has to be begun afresh. All courses or methods of human life have hitherto been failures. Some course of life is needed based on things as they are, irrespective of tradition." Yet, while maintaining that nothing was yet known, he steadfastly rejected the idea that there was anything which was actually unknowable. This indicates that he was in fact an original thinker. Nature and his literary tastes may have been the flints from which the sparks were struck, but the flames of thought were his own.

However, he had other thoughts on his mind in 1864 when, at the age of sixteen, he and his cousin Willie Cox ran away from home intent on walking through Europe to Moscow and back. They got as far as France. Perhaps once across the channel they became aware of the impracticalities of a trek of some nineteen hundred miles, ill-equipped, with no money and through lands whose languages neither boy could speak. After a week in France they returned to England. But they did not go home; tempted by rumours of cheap fares they decided to try for America. This time they got only to Liverpool, where they discovered that the cheap fares included neither food nor bedding. There was nothing for it but to return home, which they did aided by the police after young Jefferies had been discovered trying to pawn his watch for the train fare. They had been away for two weeks.

Soon after this escapade he settled to the more serious business of finding a job and in 1866 began work in Swindon as a general reporter with the *North Wilts Herald*. There was never much likelihood that Richard would work the farm, although it must have been considered. He disliked farm work — the occasions he had lent a hand had only been "for amusement." But his fascination for the land itself and all it supported was increasing with every new discovery, every fresh sensation in the fields. He later wrote to Oswald Crawfurd, then editor of the *New Quarterly*: "While at home, having very little to do, I studied Natural History from Nature — excuse the tautology. I used to take a gun for nominal occupation, and sit in the hedge for hours, noting the ways and habits even of moles and snails. I had my especial wasp-nest, and never was stung. The secret with all living things is — quiet. Be quiet and you can form a connection, so to say, with everything. . . . This went on for six or seven years — idle, you will say. Whether it was summer or winter, I would always find something to interest me . . . I was sensitive to all things, . . . to the least blade of grass, to the largest oak."

Crawfurd may not have said "idle," but a good many others did. It was well known that he would spend hours on end, day after day apparently mooning about aimlessly in the fields. He was aware that his behaviour was attracting derisive comments, and he often hid if he spied anyone approaching. Watching the tall, slightly stooping figure loafing about the fields one local sneered that Jefferies was "cut out for a gentleman — had there been any money." "That young Jefferies," warned another, "is not the sort of fellow you want hanging about in your covers." Even his own father scornfully refers to "our Dick poking about in them hedges." But there was never the slightest possibility that he would be deterred.

He often took himself to Liddington Hill, a favourite place and "the most commanding down" near his home. There he sat in deep contemplation of Nature; not thinking, but imbibing every sound and smell, every plain or intricate shape. With each visit there his empathy with nature became more acute and profound until, at the age of eighteen, his meditations culminated when he experienced a crushing intensity of feeling which was to form the cornerstone of his life. He described these overwhelming moments of ecstacy as Soul-Life. (An exact definition of this he found impossible, but he once called the Soul the "mind of the mind").

The experience is reflected either blatantly or by insinuation in nearly all his writing, but it was not until seventeen years later that he felt equal to the task of relating it in *The Story of My Heart* — and even this attempt he called "a fragment scarcely hewn." The following sentences are distilled from that book:

"I hid my face in the grass, I was wholly prostrated; I I was rapt and carried away. Involuntarily I drew a long breath, then I breathed slowly. My thought, or inner consciousness, went up through the illumined sky, and was lost in a moment of exaltation. This only lasted a very short time, perhaps only part of a second, and while it lasted there was no formulated wish. I was absorbed, I drank the beauty of the morning; I was exalted. I was plunged deep in existence, and with all that existence I prayed. Through every blade of grass in the thousand, thousand grasses; through the million leaves, veined and edge-cut, on bush and tree; through the song-notes and the marked feathers of the birds; through the insects' hum and the colour of the butterflies; through the soft warm air, the flecks of clouds dissolving — I used them all for prayer. I prayed that I might take from them all their energy, grandeur, and beauty, and gather it unto me. That my soul might be more than the cosmos of life. And losing thus my separateness of being I came to seem like a part of the whole.

"With all the intensity of feeling which exalted me, all the intense communion I held with the earth, the sun and sky, the stars hidden by the light, with the ocean — in no manner can the depth of these feelings be written — with these I prayed. The inexpressible beauty of all filled me with a rapture, an ecstacy, an inflatus. With this inflatus, too, I prayed. Just to touch the lichened bark of a tree, or the end of a spray projecting over the path as I walked, seemed to repeat the prayer in me. (The prayer) requires no waking, no renewal; it is always with me: I am it; the fact of my existence expresses it."

The words reveal Jefferies' insight pure and untarnished. "I did not then define, or analyse, or understand this," he wrote. In those same moments he also had an insight into the nature of time:

"Realizing that spirit, recognizing my own inner consciousness, the psyche, so clearly, I cannot understand time. It is eternity now. I am in the midst of it. It is about me in the sunshine; I am in it, as the butterfly floats in the light-laden air. Nothing has to come; it is now. Now is eternity; now is the immortal life. Here this moment, on earth, now; I exist in it. The years, the centuries, the cycles are absolutely nothing. To the soul there is no past and no future; all is and ever will be, in now. For artificial purposes time is agreed on, but there is really no such thing. Time has never existed, and never will. It is eternity now, it always was eternity, and always will be. By no possible means could I get into time if I tried. I am in eternity now and must there remain. Haste not, be at rest, this Now is eternity."

The Story of My Heart is a short book, and this vision of eternity — a vision realized in an instant of "no-time" — takes up several of its pages. Yet when offering the manuscript to his publisher Jefferies insisted, ". . . there are no words wasted in it. What made it all so difficult to explain was that, to Jefferies, this was no pretty but fanciful idea. To him it was not an idea at all; it was a *fact* — a mysterious fact which mere vocabulary could not properly convey. Thus his points are made by repetition rather than by concise definition; it was passion, he said, more than cold reason. In his preliminary notes, however, Jefferies seems to condense the message of the whole book into a few simple words: "You can see your soul if you hold a flower in your hand."

He returns to the motif in his essay *Wild Flowers* when he speaks of "unconscious happiness in finding flowers — unconscious and unquestioning, and therefore unbounded." But Richard Jefferies was not long to remain unquestioning. The fact he had; but *why* the fact, from *whence* the fact? There must, he thought, be something more, something Beyond.

He was conversant with the advances of science and had studied philosophy and various religious teachings. All of these, he claimed, had proved absolutely useless as a means to unfolding the Beyond. They were too specialised, too narrow in outlook; they confined the imagination until "by degrees the mind is enclosed in a husk." The slate of learning should be wiped clean and begun again. There must be *new* ideas. "Written tradition, systems of culture, modes of thought, have for me no existence," he said. "An enumeration of the useless would almost be an enumeration of everything hitherto pursued. Take a broom and sweep the (Egyptian) papyri into the dust. The Assyrian terra-cotta tablets — take a hammer and demolish them. Set a battery to beat down the pyramids, and a mind-battery to destroy the deadening influence of tradition. There is a mass of knowledge so called at the present day equally useless, and nothing but an encumbrance." Books he pronounced "useless, not equal to one bubble borne along on the running brook. The strangest people I have met are those who read books and believe in them." All previous inquiries into the ultimate basis of reality had been misguided: "The explanation not to be sought in birth, life, death, immortality; these the wrong questions."

The Rinzai sect of Zen Buddhists seek sudden enlightenment through the use of koans. (A koan is a problem or riddle that admits no logical solution; a commonly quoted example is, "What is the sound of one hand clapping?") In seeking the Beyond Richard Jefferies had set himself something in the nature of a koan.

But, however much of man's thinking Jefferies rejected, he did not reject thought itself. This is perhaps rather strange, for had not thought been responsible for all those past ideas and theories Jefferies found so reprehensible? And what part had thought played in the experiences on Liddington Hill? None at all. He had not contrived a vision of truth by dint of intellectual dexterity; at the moment of benediction thought had been entirely absent. (Incidentally, Liddington Hill was by no means the only place such feelings came to him.)

However Jefferies did not now reject thought — far from it; thought, to his mind, was the very key. There must be *new* thoughts, new ideas, new possibilities. The solution "must be dragged forth by might of thought from the immense forces of the universe." Even while on Liddington Hill, "after the sensuous enjoyment always came the thought, the desire." The sole aim of *The Story of My Heart* had been "to free thought from every trammel." But as thought entered so did anomalies in his previous assertions. He had repeatedly pronounced all books to be useless. Now he decided "the Greek and Roman philosophers have the value of furnishing the mind with material to think from."

On Liddington Hill Jefferies had felt "absorbed into the being or existence of the universe." Before long the intervention of thought began to tear asunder this sense of oneness: "By no course of reasoning, however tortuous, can nature and the universe be fitted to the mind. Nor can the mind be fitted to the cosmos. My mind cannot be twisted to it; I am separate altogether from these designless things." He continued with his thoughts, first in a spirit of high optimism, later more desperately and, sometimes, close to despair.

There is a Zen maxim which says: "Before you study Zen, mountains are mountains and river are rivers; while you are studying Zen, mountains are no longer mountains and rivers are no longer rivers; but once you have had enlightenment, mountains are once again mountains and rivers again rivers." That Jefferies found himself lodged in the second stage seems obvious — he even echoed its words: "The water was more to me than the water, and the sun than the sun." (See also *The Sun and the Brook).* He often felt himself to be "hovering on the verge of a great truth." He was very much aware of his dilemma, and in a poem never published in his lifetime he prays for an escape:

Oh, let me see beyond my mind!
Each morning I rise and see no more,
No further than I did at first;
Still to the same old thought confined,
The tyranny of the old thought. . .

Even at the end of his life when he had proved thought to be such an ill-fitting key to the Beyond, still he could not rid himself of it. "I have an inspiration," he said, "and then carefully destroy it with rationalism."

In 1867, not long after the Liddington Hill experience and only a year after joining the *North Wilts Herald*, his career was interrupted when he fell very ill and was unable to work for several months. At one stage he was barely able to walk thirty paces. His recovery might have been the sooner had it been more in his nature to relax. "I did too much yesterday in the way of study — my head when I got to bed seemed to swell big enough to fill the room." By the time he was recovered fit for work he had missed the busiest time of year at the *North Wilts Herald*, and a replacement had had to be found. He resumed work for the paper on a more or less part-time basis, hoping to supplement his income by writing local histories and melodramatic fiction. This was not a financial success and it is to his credit that he remained at this time unswervingly optimistic about his future as a writer. In September 1870 he took a short holiday in Brussels. When he returned he was virtually penniless. Knowing his parents would be displeased with his state of affairs and would chide him for his apparently devil-may-care attitude, he wrote to John Woolford, a local farmer, and begged for lodgings. "I cannot go home. I would sooner starve. I can only go home when I am independent." In return for his keep Jefferies offered to help out on Woolford's farm and, should anything remain outstanding, would make up the difference when things began to look up. The arrangement did not last long, however, and Richard was soon back at Coate.

By 1871 he was worse off than ever, even though he had written and submitted for publication all sorts of things. "Very few were rejected, but none brought any return." He was threatened for debt. As if almost to add to his problems he had fallen in love with Jessie Baden of Daye House Farm, near Coate, but could not contemplate marriage whilst in such straits.

The breakthrough came the following year. Joseph Arch had motivated the agricultural workers of several counties into forming a union. There was a strike and the farm labourers were national news. Richard Jefferies took up his pen and wrote a letter to *The Times* in support of their employers. He wrote patronisingly, perhaps sometimes absurdly about the lot of the farm labourer: "No class of persons in England receive so many attentions and benefits from their superiors." He praised the farmers: the wonder was, he said, that they had done so much for the labourer, "finding him with better cottages, better wages, better education, and affording him better opportunities of rising in the social scale." Amid the flurry of correspondence provoked by this long letter Jefferies wrote twice more to *The Times*. His main criticism of the labourer was his unwillingness to help himself. The opinions he proferred in the letters differed vastly from those he was later to declare. He came to view all forms of philanthropy with a degree of cynicism and never missed an opportunity to champion the poor: "That any human being should dare to apply to another the epithet 'pauper' is, to me, the greatest, the vilest, the most unpardonable crime that could be committed. Each human being, by mere birth, has a birthright in this earth and all its productions. . . . It matters not in the least if the poor be improvident, or drunken, or evil in any way. Food and drink, roof and clothes, are the inalienable right of every child born into the light. . . . Not as a present from philanthropy, in order that some fool may pose himself as a saint, but as a *right*."

But the most important thing about his letters to *The Times* is that they were so well written and brought Jefferies' name favourably to the attention of other editors.

Before long he was contributing agricultural articles regularly to a number of periodicals. He also persevered with his fiction writing and in 1874 his first novel, *The Scarlet Shawl*, was published. In the same year he and Jessie Baden were married. Within a further year there appeared the first essays dealing with the flora and fauna of the fields in a way not directly related to the business of farming. Demand for his work continued to grow and he was now working under pressure. In 1877, at the age of twenty-nine, he left Coate and the Wiltshire countryside for ever and moved to Surbiton to be nearer to his publishers in London. Still hoping to make his mark as a novelist, more fiction was published; many of the essays were collected into books and Jefferies became established as the leading country writer of his day. But he felt there was "little indeed in the more immediate suburbs of London to gratify the sense of the beautiful." There was a place, however, where he could retreat from the routine of house-life, the constant pressure of work and all the things which "dull the keenest edge of thought." "From my home near London," he wrote, "I made a pilgrimage almost daily to an aspen by a brook: how much I prayed and sighed there for soul-life . . . the prayer was the same as that which I felt years before on the hills." His observations at this place of meditation are written in *A Brook* and *A London Trout*. On occasions he would take the train to the Sussex downs and then beyond to that most magical and beloved of places, the sea.

In 1881 he completed work on one of his best known books, *Bevis: The Story of a Boy*. Jefferies evoked the memory of his native Coate for the book's setting, and the mind of the boy, Bevis, is an autobiographical study. As he awaited the publication of this adventure story for the young, Jefferies began drafting *The Story of My Heart*, a further autobiography of the mind but this time without recourse to fictional events. But in December 1881 he was taken ill with a fistula, probably tubercular in origin. There followed a series of painful operations, and he could do no work for a year. What little money he had managed to save was soon spent. In July 1882 he moved again, this time to Brighton for the sea air. There he improved enough to continue work on *The Story of My Heart*, though the wounds from his operations were not fully healed until 1883 and he was never again to be really well.

It had been seventeen years since "an inner and esoteric meaning" had begun to come to him "from all the visible universe." Now he was ill, but only death itself would have stilled his pen; *The Story of My Heart* would no longer be denied utterance. "Through it all," he wrote in a draft copy, "and even in the cruellest moment, the old thought continued. Something says it must be done, it must not longer be postponed, no matter how roughly or imperfectly, let it be done. I will try." The book was published in 1883.

Jefferies began to suffer from stomach pains and bouts of debilitation. He did not at the time consider his illness to be serious and attributed his symptoms to "too ceaseless work." But in 1885 his health broke down completely: the cause of his pains was found to be ulceration of the small intestine, again probably tubercular. He could now "neither lie, stand, walk, sit, without distress. The pain was awful — like lightning through the brain." There were times when he was not able even to hold a pen; some of his last, and best, work was dictated to his wife. But whenever he could he continued to fill his notebooks, mostly in preparation for an enlarged version of his autobiography. Always solitary, he now felt more isolated than ever. Even nature gave no succour. All his life he had so loved nature that now, confined to his sick-bed, he found it hard to accept that it could manage without him. But Nature did far worse than that; it offered him not the least sympathy or hope. And the realisation of this all but broke his heart. "The earth is all in all to me," he says in the essay *Hours of Spring*, "but I am nothing to the earth: it is bitter to know this before you are dead." In his notebook he put his feelings more bluntly: "I hate Nature. I turn my back on it."

Jefferies must have known that there was little chance of a recovery. Time was short and Thought still had not located and captured the Beyond. In *The Story of My Heart* he had said: "There is an immense ocean over which the mind can sail, upon which the vessel of thought has not yet been launched. I hope to launch it." In the same book he doubted the willingness of others to join him in this mission: "The complacency with which the mass of people go about their daily task, absolutely indifferent to all other considerations, is appalling in its concentrated stolidity. They do not intend wrong — they intend rightly: in truth, they work against the entire human race. So wedded and so confirmed is the world in its narrow groove of self, . . . so callous to its own possibilities, and so grown to its chains, that I almost despair to see it awakened." And earlier he had written: "Anxious to arrive at a decision upon some important matter, they lay their foreheads in their hands, shut their eyes, and call up a succession of vague images, disconnected and interrupted, and call that thinking." But he continued to hope, and when desperately ill he wrote in *Hours of Spring:* "Because my heart beats feebly today, my trickling pulse scarcely notating the passing of the time, so much the more do I hope that those to come in future years may see wider and enjoy fuller than I have done."

It is a prime function of the mind to think, to ask questions both simple and profound. Thought creates ideas, opinions, possibilities; thought criticises and refines; thought might draw conclusions or may perceive itself in error and throw the whole question open again. And our actions are the products of our thoughts. All this is inevitable. Thought must enquire, but it is perhaps not within the scope of thought to provide absolute answers — especially to the most basic questions of life. Perhaps only when thought finds itself confounded and is stilled, only then does something true, something sacred enter the consciousness. Towards the end Jefferies endorsed this view by saying of his own questions, "You cannot answer them. You can only go by the old feeling of the Ridgeway (Liddington Hill)." If only Jefferies' "vessel of thought" had been dashed and capsized, what then might the sea have revealed to him?

He had moved in 1885 from Brighton to Eltham, in 1886 to Crowborough and finally, in search of a more beneficial environment, to Goring-on-Sea, near Worthing, Sussex. But there was to be no improvement with the passing of the months. He died on 14th August, 1887. He was thirty-eight years old.

During his short life Richard Jefferies — who was so often seen walking the fields that his Wiltshire neighbours had called him an idler — had written sufficient to fill some twenty-five volumes. Despite his commonly portrayed image of an austere solitary there is a quiet humour in much of his work; he makes many jokes in his notebooks, and in his essay *The Bathing Season* he smites the Brighton sun-seekers with a positively merry malice. On the quality of his writing the poet Edward Thomas wrote: "There is not an uncommon word, nor a word in an uncommon sense, all through Jefferies' books. There are styles which are noticeable for their very lucidity and naturalness; Jefferies' is not noticeable even to this extent. There are styles more majestic, more persuasive, more bewildering, but none which so rapidly convinces the reader of its source in the heart of one of the sincerest of men." Perhaps the greatest pity was that, as so often happens, this uncompromising seeker after truth felt so alone in his search.

"No one else seems to have seen the sparkle on the brook, or heard the music at the hatch, or to have felt back through the centuries; and when I try to describe these things to them they look at me with stolid incredulity. No one seems to understand how I got food from the clouds, nor what there was in the night, nor why it is not so good to look at it out of windows. They turn their faces away from me, so that perhaps after all I was mistaken, and there never was any such place or any such meadows, and I was never there. And perhaps in course of time I shall find out also when I pass away physically, that as a matter of fact there never was any earth." Thus concludes *My Old Village*, one of his last essays. The mood is that of a man quietly reconciled to fate, but is in sharp contrast to the last pages of his notebooks. The following distillation shows him to the very end pursuing the Beyond with an urgent and poignant demand:

"I am so anxious to find a Mover Beyond, because I feel the crushing helplessness, hopelessness and the dread. The end comes at last and still ignorant. In the end I shall find out nothing, I shall only be conscious of the immensity of the problem. How densely stupid I must be to have all in front of my eyes and not see the meaning of it! Sun, moon, stars, earth, trees, man, myself — all in sight, all staring me in the face. I cannot see it for looking at it. I feel so very, very stupid: I cannot see or understand. I shall never see the end. I brood too long: for all is endless thinking, but life is not. When shall I awake — when shall I awake?"

Richard Jefferies declared his first autobiography incomplete, inadequately expressed. He made copious notes for a further volume, but his untimely death prevented its writing. No matter: the real story of his heart is encompassed in the final entry in his notebook, probably the last words ever formed by his own hand:

"I dream of Ideality."

Peter and Carol Cholerton 1982.

Under the Acorns

Coming along a woodland lane, a small round and glittering object in the brushwood caught my attention. The ground was but just hidden in that part of the wood with a thin growth of brambles, low, and more like creepers than anything else. These scarcely hid the surface, which was brown with the remnants of oak-leaves; there seemed so little cover, indeed, that a mouse might have been seen. But at that spot some great spurge-plants hung this way and that, leaning aside, as if the stems were too weak to uphold the heads of dark-green leaves. Thin grasses, perfectly white, bleached by sun and dew, stood in a bunch by the spurge; their seeds had fallen, the last dregs of sap had dried within them, there was nothing left but the bare stalks. A creeper of bramble fenced round one side of the spurge and white grass bunch, and brown leaves were visible on the surface of the ground through the interstices of the spray. It was in the midst of this little thicket that a small, dark, and glittering object caught my attention. I knew it was the eye of some creature at once, but, supposing it nothing more than a young rabbit, was passing on, thinking of other matters, when it occurred to me, before I could finish the step I had taken, so quick is thought, that the eye was not large enough to be that of a rabbit. I stopped; the black glittering eye had gone —the creature had lowered its neck, but immediately noticing that I was looking in that direction, it cautiously raised itself a little, and I saw at once that the eye was the eye of a bird. This I knew first by its size, and next by its position in relation to the head, which was invisible — for had it been a rabbit or hare, its ears would have projected. The moment after, the eye itself confirmed this — the nictitating membrane was rapidly drawn over it, and as rapidly removed. This membrane is the distinguishing mark of a bird's eye. But what bird? Although I was within two yards, I could not even see its head, nothing but the glittering eyeball, on which the light of the sun glinted. The sunbeams came over my shoulder straight into the bird's face.

Without moving — which I did not wish to do, as it would disturb the bird — I could not see its plumage; the bramble spray in front, the spurge behind, and the bleached grasses at the side, perfectly concealed it. Only two birds I considered would be likely to squat and remain quiescent like this — partridge or pheasant; but I could not contrive to view the least portion of the neck. A moment afterwards the eye came up again, and the bird slightly moved its head, when I saw its beak, and knew it was a pheasant immediately. I then stepped forward — almost on the bird — and a young pheasant rose, and flew between the tree-trunks to a deep dry watercourse, where it disappeared under some withering yellow ferns.

Of course I could easily have solved the problem long before, merely by startling the bird; but what would have been the pleasure of that? Any plough-lad could have forced the bird to rise, and would have recognised it as a pheasant; to me, the pleasure consisted in discovering it under every difficulty. That was woodcraft; to kick the bird up would have been simply nothing at all. Now I found why I could not see the pheasant's neck or body; it was not really concealed, but shaded out by the mingled hues of white grasses, the brown leaves of the surface, and the general grey-brown tints. Now it was gone, there was a vacant space — its plumage had filled up that vacant space with hues so similar, that, at no farther distance than two yards, I did not recognise it by colour. Had the bird fully carried out its instinct of concealment, and kept its head down as well as its body, I should have passed it. Nor should I have seen its head if it had looked the other way; the eye betrayed its presence. The dark glittering eye, which the sunlight touched, caught my attention instantly. There is nothing like an eye in inanimate nature; no flower, no speck on a bough, no gleaming stone wet with dew, nothing, indeed, to which it can be compared. The eye betrayed it: I could not overlook an eye. Neither nature nor inherited experience had taught the pheasant to hide its eye; the bird not only wished to conceal itself, but to watch my motions, and, looking up from its cover, was immediately observed.

At a turn of the lane there was a great heap of oak "chumps," crooked logs, sawn in lengths, and piled together. They were so crooked, it was difficult to find a seat, till I hit on one larger than the rest. The pile of "chunks" rose half-way up the stem of an oak-tree, and formed a wall of wood at my back; the oak-boughs reached over and made a pleasant shade. The sun was warm enough to render resting in the open air delicious, the wind cool enough to prevent the heat becoming too great; the pile of timber kept off the draught, so that I could stay and listen to the gentle "hush, rush" of the breeze in the oak above me; "hush" as it came slowly, "rush" as it came fast, and a low undertone as it nearly ceased. So thick were the haws on a bush of thorn opposite, that they tinted the hedge a red colour among the yellowing hawthorn-leaves. To this red hue the blackberries that were not ripe, the thick dry red sorrel stalks, a bright canker on a brier almost as bright as a rose, added their colours. Already the foliage of the bushes had been thinned, and it was possible to see through the upper parts of the boughs. The sunlight, therefore, not only touched their outer surfaces, but passed through and lit up the branches within, and the wild-fruit upon them. Though the sky was clear and blue between the clouds, that is, without mist or haze, the sunbeams were coloured the faintest yellow, as they always are on a ripe autumn day. This yellow shone back from grass and leaves, from bough and tree-trunk, and seemed to stain the ground. It is very pleasant to the eyes, a soft, delicate light, that gives another beauty to the atmosphere. Some roan cows were wandering down the lane, feeding on the herbage at the side; their colour, too, was lit up by the peculiar light, which gave a singular softness to the large shadows of the trees upon the sward. In a meadow by the wood the oaks cast broad shadows on the short velvety sward, not so sharp and definite as those of summer, but tender, and, as it were, drawn with a loving hand. They were large shadows, though it was mid-day — a sign that the sun was no longer at his greatest height, but declining. In July, they would scarcely have extended beyond the rim of the boughs; the rays would have dropped perpendicularly, now they slanted. Pleasant as it was, there was regret in the thought that the summer was going fast. Another sign — the grass by the gateway, an acre of it, was brightly yellow with hawkweeds, and under these were the last faded brown heads of meadow clover; the brown, the bright yellow discs, the green grass, the tinted sunlight falling upon it, caused a wavering colour that fleeted before the glance.

All things brown, and yellow, and red, are brought out by the autumn sun; the brown furrows freshly turned where the stubble was yesterday, the brown bark of trees, the brown fallen leaves, the brown stalks of plants; the red haws, the red unripe blackberries, red bryony berries, reddish-yellow fungi; yellow hawkweed, yellow ragwort, yellow hazel-leaves, elms, spots in lime or beech; not a speck of yellow, red, or brown the yellow sunlight does not find out. And these make autumn, with the caw of rooks, the peculiar autumn caw of laziness and full feeding, the sky blue as March between the great masses of dry cloud floating over, the mist in the distant valleys, the tinkle of traces as the plough turns, and the silence of the woodland birds. The lark calls as he rises from the earth, the swallows still wheeling call as they go over, but the woodland birds are mostly still, and the restless sparrows gone forth in a cloud to the stubble. Dry clouds, because they evidently contain no moisture that will fall as rain here; thick mists, condensed haze only, floating on before the wind. The oaks were not yet yellow, their leaves were half green, half brown; Time had begun to invade them, but had not yet indented his full mark.

Of the year there are two most pleasurable seasons: the spring, when the oak-leaves come russet-brown on the great oaks; the autumn, when the oak-leaves begin to turn. At the one, I enjoy the summer that is coming; at the other, the summer that is going. At either, there is a freshness in the atmosphere, a colour everywhere, a depth of blue in the sky, a welcome in the woods. The redwings had not yet come; the acorns were full, but still green; the greedy rooks longed to see them riper. They were very numerous, the oaks covered with them, a crop for the greedy rooks, the greedier pigeons, the pheasants, and the jays.

One thing I missed — the corn. So quickly was the harvest gathered, that those who delight in the colour of the wheat had no time to enjoy it. If any painter had been looking forward to August to enable him to paint the corn, he must have been disappointed. There was no time; the sun came, saw, and conquered, and the sheaves were swept from the field. Before yet the reapers had entered one field of ripe wheat, I did indeed for a brief evening obtain a glimpse of the richness and still beauty of an English harvest. The sun was down, and in the west a pearly grey light spread widely, with a little scarlet drawn along its lower border. Heavy shadows hung in the foliage of the elms; the clover had closed, and the quiet moths had taken the place of the humming-bees. Southwards, the full moon, a red-yellow disc, shone over the wheat, which appeared the finest pale amber. A quiver of colour — an undulation — seemed to stay in the air, left from the heated day; the sunset hues and those of the red-tinted moon fell as it were into the remnant of day, and filled the wheat; they were poured into it, so that it grew in their colours. Still heavier the shadows deepened in the elms; all was silence, save for the sound of the reapers on the other side of the hedge, slash — rustle, slash — rustle, and the drowsy night came down as softly as an eyelid.

While I sat on the log under the oak, every now and then wasps came to the crooked pieces of sawn timber, which had been barked. They did not appear to be biting it — they can easily snip off fragments of the hardest oak — they merely alighted and examined it, and went on again. Looking at them, I did not notice the lane till something moved, and two young pheasants ran by along the middle of the track and into the cover at the side. The grass at the edge which they pushed through closed behind them, and feeble as it was — grass only — it shut off the interior of the cover as firmly as iron bars. The pheasant is a strong lock upon the woods; like one of Chubb's patent locks, he closes the woods as firmly as an iron safe can be shut. Wherever the pheasant is artificially reared, and a great "head" kept up for battue-shooting, there the woods are sealed. No matter if the wanderer approach with the most harmless of intentions, it is exactly the same as if he were a species of burglar. The botanist, the painter, the student of nature, all are met with the high-barred gate and the threat of law. Of course, the pheasant-lock can be opened by the silver key; still, there is the fact, that since pheasants have been bred on so large a scale, half the beautiful woodlands of England have been fastened up. Where there is no artificial rearing there is much more freedom; those who love the forest can roam at their pleasure, for it is not the fear of damage that locks the gate, but the pheasant. In every sense, the so-called sport of battue-shooting is injurious — injurious to the sportsman, to the poorer class, to the community. Every true sportsman should discourage it, and indeed does. I was talking with a thorough sportsman recently, who told me, to my delight, that he never reared birds by hand; yet he had a fair supply, and could always give a good day's sport, judged as any reasonable man would judge sport. Nothing must enter the domains of the hand-reared pheasant; even the nightingale is not safe. A naturalist has recorded that in a district he visited, the nightingales were always shot by the keepers and their eggs smashed, because the singing of these birds at night disturbed the repose of the pheasants! Thet also always stepped on the eggs of the fern-owl, which are laid on the ground, and shot the bird if they saw it, for the same reason, as it makes a jarring sound at dusk. The fern-owl, or goat-sucker, is one of the most harmless of birds — a sort of evening swallow — living on moths, chafers, and similar night-flying insects.

Continuing my walk, still under the oaks and green acorns, I wondered why I did not meet anyone. There was a man cutting fern in the wood — a labourer — and another cutting up thistles in a field; but with the exception of men actually employed and paid, I did not meet a single person, though the lane I was following is close to several well-to-do places. I call that a well-to-do place where there are hundreds of large villas inhabited by wealthy people. It is true that the great majority of persons have to attend to business, even if they enjoy a good income; still, making every allowance for such a necessity, it is singular how few, how very few, seem to appreciate the quiet beauty of this lovely country. Somehow, they do not seem to see it — to look over it; there is no excitement in it, for one thing. They can see a great deal in Paris, but nothing in an English meadow. I have often wondered at the rarity of meeting anyone in the fields, and yet — curious anomaly — if you point out anything, or describe it, the interest exhibited is marked. Everyone takes an interest, but no one goes to see for himself. For instance, since the natural history collection was removed from the British Museum to a separate building at South Kensington, it is stated that the visitors to the Museum have fallen from an average of twenty-five hundred a day to one thousand; the inference is, that out of every twenty-five, fifteen came to see the natural history cases. Indeed, it is difficult to find a person who does not take an interest in some department of natural history, and yet I scarcely ever meet anyone in the fields. You may meet many in the autumn far away in places famous for scenery, but almost none in the meadows at home.

I stayed by a large pond to look at the shadows of the trees on the green surface of duckweed. The soft green of the smooth weed received the shadows as if specially prepared to show them to advantage. The more the tree was divided — the more interlaced its branches and less laden with foliage, the more it "came out" on the green surface; each slender twig was reproduced, and sometimes even the leaves. From an oak, and from a lime, leaves had fallen, and remained on the green weed; the flags by the shore were turning brown; a tint of yellow was creeping up the rushes, and the great trunk of a fir shone reddish brown in the sunlight. There was colour even about the still pool, where the weeds grew so thickly that the moorhens could scarcely swim through them.

The Green Corn

PURE colour almost always gives the idea of fire, or, rather, it is perhaps as if a light shone through as well as the colour itself. The fresh green blade of corn is like this — so pellucid, so clear and pure in its green as to seem to shine with colour. It is not brilliant — not a surface gleam nor an enamel — it is stained through. Beside the moist clods the slender flags arise, filled with the sweetness of the earth. Out of the darkness under — that darkness which knows no day save when the ploughshare opens its chinks — they have come to the light. To the light they have brought a colour which will attract the sunbeams from now till harvest. They fall more pleasantly on the corn, toned, as if they mingled with it. Seldom do we realize that the world is practically no thicker to us than the print of our footsteps on the path. Upon that surface we walk and act our comedy of life, and what is beneath is nothing to us. But it is out from that underworld, from the dead and the unknown, from the cold, moist ground, that these green blades have sprung. Yonder a steam-plough pants up the hill, groaning with its own strength, yet all that strength and might of wheels, and piston, and chains cannot drag from the earth one single blade like these. Force cannot make it; it must grow — an easy word to speak or write, in fact full of potency.

It is this mystery — of growth and life, of beauty and sweetness and colour, and sun-loved ways starting forth from the clods — that gives the corn its power over me. Somehow I identify myself with it; I live again as I see it. Year by year it is the same, and when I see it I feel that I have once more entered on a new life. And to my fancy, the spring, with its green corn, its violets, and hawthorn leaves, and increasing song, grows yearly dearer and more dear to this our ancient earth. So many centuries have flown. Now it is the manner with all natural things to gather as it were by smallest particles. The merest grain of sand drifts unseen into a crevice, and by-and-by another; after a while there is heap; a century and it is a mound, and then everyone observes and comments on it. Time itself has gone on like this; the years have accumulated, first in drifts, then in heaps, and now a vast mound, to which the mountains are knolls, rises up and overshadows us. Time lies heavy on the world. The old, old earth is glad to turn from the cark and care of driftless centuries to the first sweet blades of green.

There is sunshine to-day, after rain, and every lark is singing. Across the vale a broad cloud-shadow descends the hillside, is lost in the hollow, and presently, without warning, slips over the edge, crossing swiftly along the green tips. The sunshine follows — the warmer for its momentary absence. Far, far down in a grassy combe stands a solitary corn-rick, conical-roofed, casting a lonely shadow — marked because so solitary — and beyond it, on the rising slope, is a brown copse. The leafless branches take a brown tint in the sunlight; on the summit above there is furze; then more hill-lines drawn against the sky. In the tops of the dark pines at the corner of the copse, could the glance sustain itself to see them, there are finches warming themselves in the sunbeams. The thick needles shelter them from the current of air, and the sky is bluer above the pines. Their hearts are full already of the happy days to come, when the moss yonder by the beech, and the lichen on the fir-trunk, and the loose fibres caught in the fork of an unbending bough, shall furnish forth a sufficient mansion for their young. Another broad cloud-shadow, and another warm embrace of sunlight. All the serried ranks of the green corn bow at the word of command as the wind rushes over them.

There is largeness and freedom here. Broad as the down and free as the wind, the thought can roam high over the narrow roofs in the vale. Nature has affixed no bounds to thought. All the palings, and walls, and crooked fences deep down yonder are artificial. The fetters and traditions, the routine, the dull roundabout, which deadens the spirit like the cold moist earth, are the merest nothing. Here it is easy with the physical eye to look over the highest roof, which must also always be the narrowest. The moment the eye of the mind is filled with the beauty of things natural an equal freedom and width of view comes to it. Step aside from the trodden footpath of personal experience, throwing away the petty cynicism bred of petty hopes disappointed. Step out upon the broad down beside the green corn, and let its freshness become part of life. The wind passes and it bends — let the wind, too, pass over the spirit. From the cloud-shadow it emerges to the sunshine — let the heart come out from the shadow of roofs to the open glow of the sky. High above, the songs of the larks fall as rain — receive it with open hands. Pure is the colour of the green flags, the slender, pointed blades — let the thought be pure as the light that shines through that colour. Broad are the downs and open the aspect — gather the breadth and largeness of view. Never can that view be wide enough and large enough; there will always be room to aim higher. As the air of the hills enriches the blood, so let the presence of these beautiful things enrich the inner sense.

On the Downs

A TRAILING beam of light sweeps through the combe, broadening out where it touches the ground, and narrowing up to the cloud with which it travels. The hollow groove between the hills is lit up where it falls as with a ray cast from a mirror. It is an acre wide on the sward, and tapers up to the invisible slit in the cloud; a mere speck of light from the sky enlightens the earth, and one thought opens the hearts of all men. On the slope here the furze is flecked with golden spots, and black-headed stone-chats perch on ant-hills or stray flints, taking no heed of a quiet wanderer. Afar, blue line upon blue line of down is drawn along in slow curves, and beneath, the distant sea appears a dim plain with five bright streaks, where the sunshine pours through as many openings in the clouds. The wind smells like an apple fresh plucked; suddenly the great beam of light vanishes as the sun comes out, and at once the single beam is merged in the many.

Light and colour, freedom and delicious air, give exquisite pleasure to the senses; but the heart searches deeper, and draws forth food for itself from sunshine, hills and sea. Desiring their beauty so deeply, the desire in a measure satisfies itself. It is a thirst which slakes itself to grow the stronger. It springs afresh from the light, from the blue hill-line yonder, from the gorse-flower at hand; to seize upon something that seems in them, which they symbolize and speak of; to take it away within oneself; to absorb it and feel conscious of it — a something that cannot be defined, but which corresponds with all that is highest, truest, and most ideal within the mind. It says, Hope and aspire, strive for largeness of thought. The wind blows, and declares that the mind has capacity for more than has ever yet been brought to it. The wind is wide, and blows not only here, but along the whole range of hills — the hills are not broad enough for it; nor is the sea — it crosses the ocean and spreads itself whither it will. Though invisible, it is material, and yet it knows no limit. As the wind to the fixed boulder lying deep in the sward, so is the immaterial mind to the wind. There is capacity in it for more than has ever yet been placed before it. No system, no philosophy yet organized in logical sequence satisfies the inmost depth — fills and fully occupies the well of thought. Read the system, and with the last word it is over — the mind passes on and requires more. It is but a crumb tasted and gone: who should remember a crumb? But the wind blows, not one puff and then stillness: it continues; if it does cease there remains the same air to be breathed. So that the physical part of man thus always provided with air for breathing is infinitely better cared for than his mind, which gets but little crumbs, as it were, coming from old times. These are soon gone, and there remains nothing. Somewhere surely there must be more. An ancient thinker considered that the atmosphere was full of faint images — spectra, reflections, or emanations retaining shape, though without substance — that they crowded past in myriads by day and night. Perhaps there may be thoughts invisible, but floating round us, if we could only render ourselves sensitive to their impact. Such a remark must not be taken literally — it is only an effort to convey a meaning, just as shadow throws up light. The light is that there are further thoughts yet to be found.

The fullness of Nature and the vacancy of mental existence are strangely contrasted. Nature is full everywhere; there is no chink, no unfurnished space. The mind has only a few thoughts to recall, and those old, and that have been repeated these centuries past. Unless the inner mind (not that which deals with little matters of daily labour) lets itself rest on every blade of grass and leaf, and listens to the soothing wind, it must be vacant — vacant for lack of something to do, not from limit of capacity. For it is too strong and powerful for the things it has to grasp; they are crushed like wheat in a mill. It has capacity for so much, and it is supplied with so little. All the centuries that have gone have gathered hardly a bushel, as it were, and these dry grains are quickly rolled under strong thought and reduced to dust. The mill must then cease, not that it has no further power, but because the supply stops. Bring it another bushel, and it will grind as long as the grain is poured in. Let fresh images come in a stream like the apple-scented wind; there is room for them, the storehouse of the inner mind expands to receive them, wide as the sea which receives the breeze.

The Downs are now lit with sunlight — the night will cover them presently — but the mind will sigh as eagerly for these things as in the glory of day. Sooner or later there will surely come an opening in the clouds, and a broad beam of light will descend. A new thought scarcely arrives in a thousand years, but the sweet wind is always here, providing breath for the physical man. Let hope and faith remain, like the air, always, so that the soul may live. That such a higher thought may come is the desire — the prayer — which springs on viewing the blue hill line, the sea, the flower.

Stoop and touch the earth, and receive its influence; touch the flower, and feel its life; face the wind, and have its meaning; let the sunlight fall on the open hand as if you could hold it. Something may be grasped from them all, invisible yet strong. It is the sense of a wider existence — wider and higher. Illustrations drawn from material things (as they needs must be) are weak to convey such an idea. But much may be gathered indirectly by examining the powers of the mind — by the light thrown on it from physical things. Now, at this moment, the blue dome of the sky, immense as it is, is but a span to the soul. The eye-glance travels to the horizon in an instant — the soul-glance travels over all matter also in a moment. By no possibility could a world, or a series of worlds, be conceived which the mind could not traverse instantaneously. Outer space itself, therefore, seems limited and with bounds, because the mind is so penetrating it can imagine nothing to the end of which it cannot get. Space — ethereal space, as far beyond the stars as it is to them — think of it how you will, ends each side in dimness. The dimness is its boundary. The mind so instantly occupies all space that space becomes finite, and with limits. It is the things

On the Downs

that are brought before it that are limited, not the power of the mind.

The sweet wind says, again, that the inner mind has never yet been fully employed; that more than half its power still lies dormant. Ideas are the tools of the mind. Without tools you cannot build a ship. The minds of savages lie almost wholly dormant, not because naturally deficient, but because they lack the ideas — the tools — to work with. So we have had our ideas so long that we have built all we can with them. Nothing further can be constructed with these materials. But whenever new and larger materials are discovered we shall find the mind able to build much more magnificent structures. Let us, then, if we cannot yet discover them, at least wait and watch as ceaselessly as the hills, listening as the wind blows over. Three-fourths of the mind still sleeps. That little atom of it needed to conduct the daily routine of the world is, indeed, often strained to the utmost. That small part of it, again, occasionally exercised in re-learning ancient thoughts, is scarcely half employed — small as it is. There is so much more capacity in the inner mind — a capacity of which but few even dream. Until favourable times and chances bring fresh materials for it, it is not conscious of itself. Light and freedom, colour, and delicious air — sunshine, blue hill lines, and flowers — give the heart to feel that there is so much more to be enjoyed of which we walk in ignorance.

Touching a flower, it seems as if some of this were absorbed from it; it flows from the flower like its perfume. The delicate odour of the violet cannot be written; it is material yet it cannot be expressed. So there is an immaterial influence flowing from it which escapes language. Touching the greensward, there is a feeling as if the great earth sent a mystic influence through the frame. From the sweet wind, too, it comes. The sunlight falls on the hand; the light remains without on the surface, but its influence enters the very being. This sense of absorbing something from earth, and flower, and sunlight is like hovering on the verge of a great truth. It is the consciousness that a great truth is there. Not that the flower and the wind know it, but that they stir unexplored depths in the mind. They are only material — the sun sinks, darkness covers the hills, and where is their beauty then? The feeling or thought which is excited by them resides in the mind, and the purport and drift of it is a wider existence — yet to be enjoyed on earth. Only to think of and imagine it is in itself a pleasure.

The red-tipped hawthorn buds are full of such a thought; the tender green of the leaf just born speaks it. The leaf does not come forth shapeless. Already, at its emergence, there are fine divisions at the edge, markings, and veins. It is wonderful from the commencement. A thought may be put in a line, yet require a life-time to understand in its completeness. The leaf was folded in the tiny red-tipped bud — now it has come forth how long must one ponder to fully appreciate it?

Those things which are symbolized by the leaf, the flower, the very touch of earth, have not yet been put before the mind in a definite form, and shaped so that they can be weighed. The mind is like a lens. A lens can examine nothing of itself, but no matter what is put before it, it will magnify it so that it can be searched into. So whatever is put before the mind in such form that it may be perceived, the mind will search into and examine. It is not that the mind is limited, and unable to understand; it is that the facts have not yet been placed in front of it. But because as yet these things are like the leaf folded in the bud, that is no reason why we should say they are beyond hope of comprehension.

Such a course inflicts the greatest moral injury on the world. Remaining content upon a mental level is fatal, saying to ourselves, "There is nothing more, this is our limit; we can go no farther," is the ruin of the mind, as much sleep is the ruin of the body. Looking back through history, it is evident that thought has forced itself out on the world by its own power and against an immense inertia. Thought has worked its way by dint of its own energy, and not because it was welcomed. So few care or hope for a higher mental level; the old terrace of mind will do; let us rest; be assured no higher terrace exists. Experience, however, from time to time has proved that higher terraces did exist. Without doubt there are others now. Somewhere behind the broad beam of life sweeping so beautifully through the combe, somewhere behind the flower, and in the wind. Yet to come up over the blue hill line, there are deeper, wider thoughts still. Always let us look higher, in spite of the narrowness of daily life. The little is so heavy that it needs a strong effort to escape it. The littleness of daily routine; the care felt and despised, the minutiæ which grow against our will, come in time to be heavier than lead. There should be some comfort in the thought that, however these may strain the mind, it is certain that hardly a fiftieth part of its real capacity is occupied with them. There is an immense power in it unused. By stretching one muscle too much it becomes overworked; still, there are a hundred other muscles in the body. In truth, we do not fully understand our own earth, our own life, yet. Never, never let us permit the weight of little things to bear us wholly down. If any object that these are vague aspirations, so is the wind vague, yet it is real. They may direct us as strongly as the wind presses on the sails of a ship.

The blue hill line arouses a perception of a current of thought which lies for the most part unrecognized within — an unconscious thought. By looking at this blue hill line this dormant power within the mind becomes partly visible; the heart wakes up to it.

The intense feeling caused by the sunshine, by the sky, by the flowers and distant sea is an increased consciousness of our own life. The stream of light — the rush of sweet wind — excites a deeper knowledge of the soul. An unutterable desire at once arises for more of this; let us receive more of the inner soul life which seeks and sighs for purest beauty. But the word beauty is poor to convey the feelings intended. Give us the thoughts which correspond with the feeling called up by the sky, the sea afar, and the flower at hand. Let us really be in ourselves the sunbeam which we use as an illustration. The recognition of its loveliness, and of the delicious air, is really a refined form of prayer — the purer because it is not associated with any object, because of its width and openness. It is not prayer in the sense of a benefit desired, it is a feeling of rising to a nobler existence.

It does not include wishes connected with routine and labour. Nor does it depend on the brilliant sun — this mere clod of earth will cause it, even a little crumble of mould. The commonest form of matter thus regarded excites the highest form of spirit. The feelings may be received from the least morsel of brown earth adhering to the surface of the skin on the hand that has touched the ground. Inhaling this deep feeling, the soul, perforce, must pray — a rude imperfect word to express the aspiration

— with every glimpse of sunlight, whether it come in a room amid routine, or in the solitude of the hills; with every flower, and grass-blade, and the vast earth underfoot; with the gleam on the distant sea, with the song of the lark on high, and the thrush lowly in the hawthorn.

From the blue hill lines, from the dark copses on the ridges, the shadows in the combes, from the apple-sweet wind and rising grasses, from the leaf issuing out of the bud to question the sun — there comes from all of these an influence which forces the heart to lift itself in earnest and purest desire.

The soul knows itself, and would live its own life.

The Breeze on Beachy Head

THE waves coming round the promontory before the west wind still give the idea of a flowing stream, as they did in Homer's days. Here beneath the cliff, standing where beach and sand meet, it is still; the wind passes six hundred feet overhead. But yonder, every larger wave rolling before the breeze breaks over the rocks; a white line of spray rushes along them, gleaming in the sunshine; for a moment the dark rock-wall disappears, till the spray sinks.

The sea seems higher than the spot where I stand, its surface on a higher level — raised like a green mound — as if it could burst in and occupy the space up to the foot of the cliff in a moment. It will not do so, I know; but there is an infinite possibility about the sea; it may do what it is not recorded to have done. It is not to be ordered, it may overleap the bounds human observation has fixed for it. It has a potency unfathomable. There is still something in it not quite grasped and understood — something still to be discovered — a mystery.

So the white spray rushes along the low broken wall of rocks, the sun gleams on the flying fragments of the wave, again it sinks, and the rhythmic motion holds the mind, as an invisible force holds back the tide. A faith of expectancy, a sense that something may drift up from the unknown, a large belief in the unseen resources of the endless space out yonder, soothes the mind with dreamy hope.

The little rules and little experiences, all the petty ways of narrow life, are shut off behind by the ponderous and impassable cliff; as if we had dwelt in the dim light of a cave, but coming out at last to look at the sun, a great stone had fallen and closed the entrance, so that there was no return to the shadow. The impassable precipice shuts off our former selves of yesterday, forcing us to look out over the sea only, or up to the deeper heaven.

These breadths draw out the soul; we feel that we have wider thoughts than we knew; the soul has been living, as it were, in a nutshell, all unaware of its own power, and now suddenly finds freedom in the sun and the sky. Straight, as if sawn down from turf to beach, the cliff shuts off the human world, for the sea knows no time and no era; you cannot tell what century it is from the face of the sea. A Roman trireme suddenly rounding the white edge-line of chalk, borne on wind and oar from the Isle of Wight towards the grey castle at Pevensey (already old in olden days), would not seem strange. What wonder could surprise us coming from the wonderful sea?

The little rills winding through the sand have made an islet of a detached rock by the beach; limpets cover it, adhering like rivet-heads. In the stillness here, under the roof of the wind so high above, the sound of the sand draining itself is audible. From the cliff blocks of chalk have fallen, leaving hollows as when a knot drops from a beam. They lie crushed together at the base, and on the point of this jagged ridge a wheatear perches.

There are ledges three hundred feet above, and from these now and then a jackdaw glides out and returns again to his place, where, when still and with folded wings, he is but a speck of black. A spire of chalk still higher stands out from the wall, but the rains have got behind it and will cut the crevice deeper and deeper into its foundation. Water, too, has carried the soil from under the turf at the summit over the verge, forming brown streaks.

Upon the beach lies a piece of timber, part of a wreck; the wood is torn and the fibres rent where it was battered against the dull edge of the rocks. The heat of the sun burns, thrown back by the dazzling chalk; the river of ocean flows ceaselessly, casting the spray over the stones; the unchanged sky is blue.

Let us go back and mount the steps at the Gap, and rest on the sward there. I feel that I want the presence of grass. The sky is a softer blue, and the sun genial now the eye and the mind alike are relieved — the one of the strain of too great solitude (not the solitude of the woods), the other of too brilliant and hard a contrast of colours. Touch but the grass, and the harmony returns; it is repose after exaltation.

A vessel comes round the promontory; it is not a trireme of old Rome, nor the "fair and stately galley" Count Arnaldus hailed with its seamen singing the mystery of the sea. It is but a brig in ballast, high out of the water, black of hull and dingy of sail: still, it is a ship, and there is always an interest about a ship. She is so near, running along but just outside the reef, that the deck is visible. Up rises her stern as the billows come fast and roll under; then her bow lifts, and immediately she rolls, and, loosely swaying with the sea, drives along.

The slope of the billow now behind her is white with the bubbles of her passage, rising, too, from her rudder. Steering athwart with a widening angle from the land, she is laid to clear the distant point of Dungeness. Next, a steamer glides forth, unseen till she passed the cliff; and thus each vessel that comes from the westward has the charm of the unexpected. Eastward there is many a sail working slowly into the wind, and as they approach talking in the language of flags with the watch on the summit of the Head.

Once now and then the great *Orient* pauses on her outward route to Australia, slowing her engines: the immense length of her hull contains every adjunct of modern life; science, skill, and civilization are there. She starts, and is lost sight of round the cliff, gone straight away for the very ends of the world. The incident is forgotten, when one morning, as you turn over the newspaper, there is the *Orient* announced to start again. It is like a tale of enchantment; it seems but yesterday that the Head hid her from view; you have scarcely moved, attending to the daily routine of life, and scarce recognize that time has passed at all. In so few hours has the earth been encompassed.

The seagulls as they settle on the surface ride high out of the water, like the mediæval caravals, with their sterns almost as tall as the masts. Their unconcerned flight, with crooked wings unbent, as if it were no matter to them whether they flew or floated, in its peculiar jerking motion somewhat reminds one of the lapwing — the heron has it, too, a little — as if aquatic or waterside birds had a common and distinct action of the wing.

Sometimes a porpoise comes along, but just beyond the reef; looking down on him from the verge of the cliff, his course can be watched. His dark body, wet and oily, appears on the surface for two seconds; and then, throwing up his tail like the fluke of an anchor, down he goes. Now look forward, along the waves, some fifty yards or so, and he will come up, the sunshine gleaming on the water as it runs off his back, to again dive, and reappear after a similar interval. Even when the eye can no longer distinguish the form, the spot where he rises is visible, from the slight change in the surface.

The hill receding in hollows leaves a narrow plain between the foot of the sward and the cliff; it is ploughed, and the teams come to the footpath which follows the edge; and thus those who plough the sea and those who plough the land look upon each other. The one sees the vessel change her tack, the other notes the plough turning at the end of the furrow. Bramble bushes project over the dangerous wall of chalk, and grasses fill up the interstices, a hedge suspended in air; but be careful not to reach too far for the blackberries.

The green sea is on the one hand, the yellow stubble on the other. The porpoise dives along beneath, the sheep graze above. Green seaweed lines the reef over which the white spray flies, blue lucerne dots the field. The pebbles of the beach seen from the height mingle in a faint blue tint, as if the distance ground them into coloured sand. Leaving the footpath now, and crossing the stubble to "France", as the wide open hollow in the down is called by the shepherds, it is no easy matter in dry summer weather to climb the steep turf to the furze line above.

Dry grass is as slippery as if it were hair, and the sheep have fed it too close for a grip of the hand. Under the furze (still far from the summit) they have worn a path — a narrow ledge, cut by their cloven feet — through the sward. It is time to rest; and already, looking back, the sea has extended to an indefinite horizon. This climb of a few hundred feet opens a view of so many miles more. But the ships lose their individuality and human character; they are so far, so very far, away, they do not take hold of the sympathies; they seem like sketches — cunningly executed, but only sketches — on the immense canvas of the ocean. There is something unreal about them.

On a calm day, when the surface is smooth as if the brimming ocean had been straked — the rod passed across the top of the measure, thrusting off the irregularities of wave; when the distant green from long simmering under the sun becomes pale; when the sky, without cloud, but with some slight haze in it, likewise loses its hue, and the two so commingle in the pallor of heat that they cannot be separated — then the still ships appear suspended in space. They are as much held from above as upborne from beneath.

They are motionless, midway in space — whether it is sea or air is not to be known. They neither float nor fly, they are suspended. There is no force in the flat sail, the mast is lifeless, the hull without impetus. For hours they linger, changeless as the constellations, still, silent, motionless, phantom vessels on a void sea.

Another climb up from the sheep path, and it is not far then to the terrible edge of that tremendous cliff which rises straighter than a ship's side out of the sea, six hundred feet above the detached rock below, where the

The Breeze on Beachy Head

limpets cling like rivet-heads, and the sand rills run around it. But it is not possible to look down to it — the glance of necessity falls outwards, as a raindrop from the eaves is deflected by the wind, because it *is* the edge where the mould crumbles; the rootlets of the grass are exposed; the chalk is about to break away in flakes.

You cannot lean over as over a parapet, lest such a flake should detach itself — lest a mere trifle should begin to fall, awakening a dread and dormant inclination to slide and finally plunge like it. Stand back; the sea there goes out and out, to the left and to the right, and how far is it to the blue overhead? The eye must stay here a long period, and drink in these distances, before it can adjust the measure, and know exactly what it sees.

The vastness conceals itself, giving us no landmark or milestone. The fleck of cloud yonder, does it part it in two, or is it but a third of the way? The world is an immense cauldron, the ocean fills it, and we are merely on the rim — this narrow land is but a ribbon to the limitlessness yonder. The wind rushes out upon it with wild joy; springing from the edge of the earth, it leaps out over the ocean. Let us go back a few steps and recline on the warm, dry turf.

It is pleasant to look back upon the green slope and the hollows and narrow ridges, with sheep and stubble and some low hedges, and oxen, and that old, old sloth — the plough — creeping in his path. The sun is bright on the stubble and the corners of furze; there are bees humming yonder, no doubt, and flowers, and hares crouching — the dew dried from around them long since, and waiting for it to fall again; partridges, too, corn-ricks, and the roof of a farmhouse by them. Lit with sunlight are the fields, warm autumn garnering all that is dear to the heart of man, blue heaven above — how sweet the wind comes from these! — the sweeter for the knowledge of the profound abyss behind.

Here, reclining on the grass — the verge of the cliff rising a little, shuts out the actual sea — the glance goes forth into the hollow unsupported. It is sweeter towards the corn-ricks, and yet the mind will not be satisfied, but ever turns to the unknown. The edge and the abyss recall us; the boundless plain, for it appears solid as the waves are levelled by distance, demands the gaze. But with use it becomes easier, and the eye labours less. There is a promontory standing out from the main wall, whence you can see the side of the cliff, getting a flank view, as from a tower.

The jackdaws occasionally floating out from the ledge are as mere specks from above, as they were from below. The reef running out from the beach, though now covered by the tide, is visible as you look down on it through the water; the seaweed, which lay matted and half dry on the rocks, is now under the wave. Boats have come round, and are beached; how helplessly little they seem beneath the cliff by the sea!

On returning homewards towards Eastbourne stay awhile by the tumulus on the slope. There are others hidden among the furze; butterflies flutter over them, and the bees hum round by day; by night the night-hawk passes, coming up from the fields and even skirting the sheds and houses below. The rains beat on them, and the storm drives the dead leaves over their low green domes; the waves boom on the shore far down.

How many times has the morning star shone yonder in the East? All the mystery of the sun and of the stars centres around these lowly mounds.

But the glory of these glorious Downs is the breeze. The air in the valleys immediately beneath them is pure and pleasant; but the least climb, even a hundred feet, puts you on a plane with the atmosphere itself, uninterrupted by so much as the tree-tops. It is the air without admixture. If it comes from the south, the waves refine it; if inland, the wheat and flowers and grass distil it. The great headland and the whole rib of the promontory is wind-swept and washed with air; the billows of the atmosphere roll over it.

The sun searches out every crevice amongst the grass, nor is there the smallest fragment of surface which is not sweetened by air and light. Underneath, the chalk itself is pure, and the turf thus washed by wind and rain, sun-dried and dew-scented, is a couch prepared with thyme to rest on. Discover some excuse to be up there always, to search for stray mushrooms — they will be stray, for the the crop is gathered extremely early in the morning — or to make a list of flowers and grasses; to do anything, and, if not, go always without any pretext. Lands of gold have been found, and lands of spices and precious merchandise; but this is the land of health.

There is the sea below to bathe in, the air of the sky up hither to breathe, the sun to infuse the invisible magnetism of his beams. These are the three potent medicines of nature, and they are medicines that by degrees strengthen not only the body but the unquiet mind. It is not necessary to always look out over the sea. By strolling along the slopes of the ridge a little way inland there is another scene where hills roll on after hills till the last and largest hides those that succeed behind it.

Vast cloud-shadows darken one, and lift their veil from another; like the sea, their tint varies with the hue of the sky over them. Deep narrow valleys — lanes in the hills — draw the footsteps downwards into their solitude, but there is always the delicious air, turn whither you will, and there is always the grass, the touch of which refreshes. Though not in sight, it is pleasant to know that the sea is close at hand, and that you have only to mount to the ridge to view it. At sunset the curves of the shore westward are filled with a luminous mist.

Or if it should be calm, and you should like to look at the massive headland from the level of the sea, row out a mile from the beach. Eastwards a bank of red vapour shuts in the sea, the wavelets — no larger than those raised by the oar — on that side are purple as if wine had been spilt upon them, but westwards the ripples shimmer with palest gold.

The sun sinks behind the summit of the Downs, and slender streaks of purple are drawn along above them. A shadow comes forth from the cliff; a duskiness dwells on the water; something tempts the eye upwards, and near the zenith there is a star.

Nature and Books

WHAT is the colour of the dandelion? There are many dandelions: that which I mean flowers in May, when the meadow-grass has started and the hares are busy by daylight. That which flowers very early in the year has a thickness of hue, and is not interesting; in autumn the dandelions quite change their colour and are pale. The right dandelion for this question is the one that comes about May with a very broad disc, and in such quantities as often to cover a whole meadow. I used to admire them very much in the fields of Surbiton (strong clay soil), and also on the towing-path of the Thames where the sward is very broad, opposite Long Ditton; indeed, I have often walked up that towing-path on a beautiful sunny morning, when all was quiet except the nightingales in the Palace hedge, on purpose to admire them. I dare say they are all gone now for evermore; still, it is a pleasure to look back on anything beautiful. What colour is this dandelion? It is not yellow, nor orange, nor gold; put a sovereign on it and see the difference. They say the gipsies call it the Queen's great hairy dog-flower — a number of words to one stalk; and so, to get a colour to it, you may call it the yellow-gold-orange plant. In the winter, on the black mud under a dark, dripping tree, I found a piece of orange peel, lately dropped — a bright red orange speck in the middle of the blackness. It looked very beautiful, and instantly recalled to my mind the great dandelion discs in the sunshine of summer. Yet certainly they are not red-orange. Perhaps, if ten people answered this question, they would each give different answers. Again, a bright day or a cloudy, the presence of a slight haze, or the juxtaposition of other colours, alters it very much; for the dandelion is not a glazed colour, like the buttercup, but sensitive. It is like a sponge, and adds to its own hue that which is passing, sucking it up.

The shadows of the trees in the wood, why are they blue? Ought they not to be dark? Is it really blue, or an illusion? And what is their colour when you see the shadow of a tall trunk aslant in the air like a leaning pillar? The fallen brown leaves wet with dew have a different brown from those that are dry, and the upper surface of the green growing leaf is different from the under surface. The yellow butterfly, if you meet one in October, has so toned down his spring yellow that you might fancy him a pale green leaf floating along the road. There is a shining, quivering, gleaming; there is a changing, fluttering, shifting; there is a mixing, weaving — varnished wings, translucent wings, wings with dots and veins, all playing over the purple heath; a very tangle of many-toned lights and hues. Then come the apples: if you look upon them from an upper window, so as to glance along the level plane of the fruit, delicate streaks of scarlet, like those that lie parallel to the eastern horizon before sunrise; golden tints under bronze, and apple-green, and some that the wasps have hollowed, more glowingly beautiful than the rest; sober leaves and black and white swallows: to see it you must be high up, as if the apples were strewn on a sward of foliage. So have I gone in three steps from May dandelion to September apple; an immense space measured by things beautiful, so filled that ten folio volumes could not hold the description of them, and I have left out the meadows, the brooks, and hills. Often in writing about these things I have felt very earnestly my own incompetence to give the least idea of their brilliancy and many-sided colours. My gamut was so very limited in its terms, and would not give a note to one in a thousand of those I saw. At last I said, I will have more words; I will have more terms; I will have a book on colour, and I will find and use the right technical name for each one of these lovely tints. I was told that the very best book was by Chevreul, which had tinted illustrations, chromatic scales, and all that could be desired.

Quite true, all of it; but for me it contained nothing. There was a good deal about assorted wools, but nothing about leaves; nothing by which I could tell you the difference between the light scarlet of one poppy and the deep purple-scarlet of another species. The dandelion remained unexplained; as for the innumerable other flowers, and wings, and sky-colours, they were not even approached. The book, in short, dealt with the artificial and not with nature. Next I went to science — works on optics, such a mass of them. Some I had read in old time, and turned to again; some I read for the first time, some translated

CHOLERTON 82

from the German, and so on. It appeared that, experimenting with physical colour, tangible paint, they had found out that red, yellow, and blue were the three primary colours; and then, experimenting with light itself, with colours not tangible, they found out that red, green, and violet were the three primary colours; but neither of these would do for the dandelion. Once upon a time I had taken an interest in spectrum analysis, and the theory of the polarization of light was fairly familiar; any number of books, but not what I wanted to know. Next the idea occurred to me of buying all the colours used in painting, and tinting as many pieces of paper a separate hue, and so comparing these with petals, and wings, and grass, and trifolium. This did not answer at all; my unskilful hands made a very poor wash, and the yellow paper set by a yellow petal did not agree, scientific reason of which I cannot enter into now. Secondly, the names attached to many of these paints are unfamiliar to general readers; it is doubtful if bistre, Leicht's blue, oxide of chromium, and so on, would convey an idea. They might as well be Greek symbols: no use to attempt to describe hues of heath or hill in that way. These, too, are only distinct colours. What was to be done with all the shades and tones? Still there remained the language of the studio; without doubt a master of painting could be found who would quickly supply the technical term of anything I liked to show him; but again no use, because it would be technical. And a still more unsurmountable difficulty occurs: in so far as I have looked at pictures, it seems as if the artists had met with the same obstacle in paints as I have in words — that is to say, a deficiency. Either painting is incompetent to express the extreme beauty of nature, or in some way the canons of art forbid the attempt.

Therefore I had to turn back, throw down my books with a bang, and get me to a bit of fallen timber in the open air to meditate.

The power of language has been gradually enlarging for a great length of time, and I venture to say that the English language at the present time can express more, and is more subtle, flexible, and, at the same time, vigorous, than any of which we possess a record. When people talk to me about studying Sanscrit, or Greek, or Latin, or German, or, still more absurd, French, I feel as if I could fell them with a mallet happily. Study the English, and you will find everything there, I reply. With such a language I fully anticipate, in years to come, a great development in the power of expressing thoughts and feelings which are now thoughts and feelings only. How many have said of the sea, "It makes me feel something I cannot say!" Hence it is clear there exists in the intellect a layer, if I may so call it, of thought yet dumb — chambers within the mind which require the key of new words to unlock. Whenever that is done a fresh impetus is given to human progress. There are a million books, and yet with all their aid I cannot tell you the colour of the May dandelion. There are three greens at this moment in my mind: that of the leaf of the flower-de-luce, that of the yellow iris leaf, and that of the bayonet-like leaf of the common flag. With admission to a million books, how am I to tell you the difference between these tints? So many, many books, and such a very, very little bit of nature in them! Though we have been so many thousand years upon the earth we do not seem to have done any more as yet than walk along beaten footpaths, and sometimes really it would seem as if there were something in the minds of many men quite artificial, quite distinct from the sun and trees and hills — altogether house people, whose gods must be set in four-cornered buildings. There is nothing in books that touches my dandelion.

It grows, ah yes, it grows! How does it grow? Builds itself up somehow of sugar and starch, and turns mud into bright colour and dead earth into food for bees, and some day perhaps for you, and knows when to shut its petals, and how to construct the brown seeds to float with the wind, and how to please the children, and how to puzzle me. Ingenious dandelion! If you find out that its correct botanical name is *Leontodon taraxacum*, or *Leontodon dens-leonis*, that will bring it into botany; and there is a place called Dandelion Castle in Kent, and a bell with the inscription:

John de Dandelion with his great dog
Brought over this bell on a mill cog –

which is about as relevant as the mere words *Leontodon taraxacum*. Botany is the knowledge of plants according to the accepted definition; naturally, therefore, when I began to think I would like to know a little more of flowers than could be learned by seeing them in the fields, I went to botany. Nothing could be more simple. You buy a book which first of all tells you how to recognize them, how to classify them; next instructs you in their uses, medical or economical; next tells you about the folk-lore and curious associations; next enters into a lucid explanation of the physiology of the plant and its relation to other creatures; and finally, and most important, supplies you with the ethical feeling, the ideal aspiration to be identified with each particular flower. One moderately thick volume would probably suffice for such a modest round as this.

Lo! now the labour of Hercules when he set about bringing up Cerberus from below, and all the work done by Apollo in the years when he ground corn, are but a little matter compared with the attempt to master botany. Great minds have been at it these two thousand years, and yet we are still only nibbling at the edge of the leaf, as the ploughboys bite the young hawthorn in spring. The mere classification — all plant-lore was a vast chaos till there came the man of Sweden, the great Linnæus, till the sexes were recognized, and everything was ruled out and set in place again. A wonderful man! I think it would be true to say it was Linnæus who set the world on its present twist of thinking, and levered our mental globe a little more perpendicular to the ecliptic. He actually gathered the dandelion and took it to bits like a scientific child; he touched nature with his fingers instead of sitting looking out of a window — perhaps the first man who had ever done so for seventeen hundred years or so, since superstition blighted the progress of pagan Rome. The work he did! But no one reads Linnæus now; the folios, indeed, might moulder to dust without loss, because his spirit has got into the minds of men, and the text is of little consequence. The best book he wrote to read now is the delightful *Tour in Lapland*, with its quaint pen-and-ink sketches, so realistically vivid, as if the thing sketched had been banged on the paper and so left its impress. I have read it three times, and I still cherish the old yellow pages; it is the best botanical book, written by the greatest of botanists, specially sent on a botanical expedition, and it contains nothing about botany. It tells you about the canoes, and the hard cheese, and the Laplander's warehouse on top of a pole, like a pigeon-house; and the innocent way in which the maiden helped the traveller in his bath, and how the aged men ran so fast that the devil could not catch them; and, best of all, because it gives a smack in the face to modern pseudo-scientific medical cant about hygiene, showing how the Laplanders break every "law," human and "divine," ventilation, bath, and diet — all the trash — and therefore enjoy the most excellent health, and live to a great old age. Still I have not succeeded in describing the immense labour there was in learning to distinguish plants on the Linnæan system. Then comes in order of time the natural system, the geographical distribution; then there is the geological relationship, so to say, to Pliocene plants, natural selection and evolution. Of that let us say nothing; let sleeping dogs lie, and evolution is a very weary dog. Most charming, however, will be found the later studies of naturalists on the interdependence of flowers and insects; there is another work the dandelion has got to do — endless, endless botany! Where did the plants come from at first? Did they come creeping up out of the sea at the edge of the estuaries, and gradually run their roots into the ground, and so make green the earth? Did Man come out of the sea, as the Greeks thought? There are so many ideas in plants. Flora, with a full lap, scattering knowledge and flowers together; everything good and sweet seems to come out of flowers, up to the very highest thoughts of the soul, and we carry them daily to the very threshold of the other world. Next you may try the microscope and its literature, and find the crystals in the rhubarb.

I remember taking sly glances when I was a very little boy at an old Culpepper's Herbal, heavily bound in leather and curiously illustrated. It was so deliciously wicked to read about the poisons; and I thought perhaps it was a book like that, only in papyrus rolls, that was used by the sorceress who got ready the poisoned mushrooms in old Rome. Youth's ideas are so imaginative, and bring together things that are so widely separated. Conscience told me I had no business to read about poisons; but there was a fearful fascination in hemlock, and I recollect tasting a little bit — it was very nasty. At this day, nevertheless, if anyone wishes to begin a pleasant, interesting, unscientific acquaintance with English plants, he would do very well indeed to get a good copy of Culpepper. Grey hairs had insisted in showing themselves in my beard when, all those weary years afterwards, I thought I would like to buy the still older Englishman, Gerard, who had no Linnæus to guide him, who walked about our English lanes centuries ago. What wonderful scenes he must have viewed when they were all a tangle of wild flowers, and plants that are now scarce were common, and the old ploughs, and the curious customs, and the wild red-deer — it would make a good picture, it really would, Gerard studying English orchids! Such a volume! — hundreds of pages, yellow of course, close type, and marvellously well printed. The minute care they must have taken in those early days of printing to get up such a book — a wonderful volume both in bodily shape and contents. Just then the only copy I could hear of was much damaged. The cunning old bookseller said he could make it up; but I have no fancy for patched books, they are not genuine; I would rather have them deficient; and the price was rather long, so I went Gerardless. Of folk-lore and medicinal use and history and associations here you have hints. The bottom of the sack is not yet; there are the monographs, years of study expended upon one species of plant growing in one locality, perhaps; some made up into thick books and some into broad quarto pamphlets, with most beautiful plates, that, if you were to see them, would tempt you to cut them out and steal them, all sunk and lost like dead ships under the sand; piles of monographs. There are warehouses in London that are choked to the beams of the roof with them, and every fresh exploration furnishes another shelf-load. The source of the Nile was unknown a very few years ago, and now, I have no doubt, there are dozens of monographs on the flowers that flourish there. Indeed, there is not a thing that grows that may not furnish a monograph. The author spends perhaps twenty years in collecting his material, during which time he must of course come across a great variety of amusing information, and then he spends another ten years writing out a fair copy of his labours. Then he thinks it does not quite do in that form, so he snips a paragraph out of the beginning and puts it at the end; next he shifts some more matter from the middle to the preface; then he thinks it over. It seems to him that it is too big, it wants condensation. The scientific world will say he has made too much of it; it ought to read very slight, and present the facts while concealing the labour. So he sets about removing the superfluous — leaves out all the personal observations, and all the little adventures he has met with in his investigations; and so, having got it down to the dry bones and stones thereof, and omitted all the mortar that stuck them together, he sends for the engraver, and the next three years are occupied in working up the illustrations. About this time some new discovery is made by a foreign observer, which necessitates a complete revision of the subject: and so having shifted the contents of the book about hither and thither till he does not know which is the end and which is the beginning, he pitches the much-mutilated copy into a drawer and turns the key. Farewell, no more of this; his declining days shall be spent in peace. A few months afterwards a work is announced in Leipsic which "really trenches on my favourite subject, and really after spending a lifetime I can't stand it." By this time his handwriting has become so shaky he can hardly read it himself, so he sends in despair for a lady who works a typewriter, and with infinite patience she makes a clean manuscript of the muddled mass. To the press at last, and the proofs come rapidly. Such a relief! How joyfully easy a thing is when you set about it! but by-and-by this won't do. Sub-section A ought to be in a footnote, family B is doubtful; and so the corrections grow and run over the margin in a thin treble hand, till they approach the bulk of the original book — a good profit for the printer; and so after about forty years the monograph is published — the work of a life is accomplished. Fifty copies are sent round to as many public libraries and learned societies, and the rest of the impression lies on the shelves till dust and time and spiders' webs have buried it. Splendid work in it too. Looked back upon from today with the key of modern thought, these monographs often contain a whole chest of treasure. And still there are the periodicals, a century of magazines and journals and reviews and notices that have been coming out these hundred years and dropping to the ground like dead leaves unnoticed. And then there are the art works — books about shape and colour and ornament, and a naturalist lately has been trying to see how the leaves of one tree look fitted on the boughs of another.

Boundless is the wealth of Flora's lap; the ingenuity of man has been weaving wreaths out of it for ages, and still the bottom of the sack is not yet. Nor have we got much news of the dandelion. For I sit on the thrown timber under the trees and meditate, and I want something more: I want the soul of the flowers.

The bee and the butterfly take their pollen and their honey, and the strange moths so curiously coloured, like the curious colouring of the owls, come to them by night, and they turn towards the sun and live their little day, and their petals fall, and where is the soul when the body decays? I want the inner meaning and the understanding of the wild flowers in the meadow. Why are they? What end? What purpose? The plant knows, and sees, and feels; where is its mind when the petal falls? Absorbed in the universal dynamic force, or what? They make no shadow of pretence, these beautiful flowers, of being beautiful for my sake, of bearing honey for me; in short, there does not seem to be any kind of relationship between us, and yet — as I said just now — language does not express the dumb feelings of the mind any more than the flower can speak. I want to know the soul of the flowers, but the word soul does not in the smallest degree convey the meaning of my wish. It is quite inadequate; I must hope that you will grasp the drift of my meaning. All these life-laboured monographs, these classifications, works of Linnæus, and our own classic Darwin, microscope, physiology, and the flower has not given us its message yet. There are a million books; there are no books: all the books have to be written. What a field! A whole million of books have got to be written. In this sense there are hardly a dozen of them done, and these mere primers. The thoughts of man are like the foraminifera, those minute shells which build up the solid chalk hills and lay the level plain of endless sand; so minute that, save with a powerful lens, you would never imagine the dust on your fingers to be more than dust. The thoughts of man are like these:

each to him seems great in his day, but the ages roll, and they shrink till they become triturated dust, and you might, as it were, put a thousand on your thumb-nail. They are not shapeless dust for all that; they are organic, and they build up and weld and grow together, till in the passage of time they will make a new earth and a new life. So I think I may say there are no books; the books are yet to be written.

Men's minds all over the printing-press world are unlearning the falsehoods that have bound them down so long; they are unlearning, the first step to learn. They are going down to nature and taking up the clods with their own hands, and so coming to have touch of that which is real. As yet we are in the fact stage; by-and-by we shall come to the alchemy, and get the honey for the inner mind and soul. I found, therefore, from the dandelion that there were no books, and it came upon me, believe me, as a great surprise, for I had lived quite certain that I was surrounded with them. It is nothing but unlearning, I find now; five thousand books to unlearn.

Then to unlearn the first ideas of history, of science, of social institutions, to unlearn one's own life and purpose; to unlearn the old mode of thought and way of arriving at things; to take off peel after peel, and so get by degrees slowly towards the truth — thus writing as it were, a sort of floating book in the mind, almost remaking the soul. It seems as if the chief value of books is to give us something to unlearn. Sometimes I feel indignant at the false views that were instilled into me in early days, and then again I see that that very indignation gives me a moral life. I hope in the days to come future thinkers will unlearn us, and find ideas infinitely better.

A Brook

Some low wooden rails guarding the approach to a bridge over a brook one day induced me to rest under an aspen, with my back against the tree. Some horse-chestnuts, beeches, and alders grew there, fringing the end of a long plantation of willow stoles which extended in the rear following the stream. In front, southwards, there were open meadows and cornfields, over which shadow and sunshine glided in succession as the sweet westerly wind carried the white clouds before it.

The brimming brook, as it wound towards me through the meads, seemed to tremble on the verge of overflowing, as the crown of wine in a glass rises yet does not spill. Level with the green grass, the water gleamed as though polished where it flowed smoothly, crossed with the dark shadows of willows which leaned over it. By the bridge, where the breeze rushed through the arches, a ripple flashed back the golden rays. The surface by the shore slipped towards a side hatch and passed over in a liquid curve, clear and unvarying, as if of solid crystal, till shattered on the stones, where the air caught up and played with the sound of the bubbles as they broke.

Beyond the green slope of corn, a thin, soft vapour hung on the distant woods, and hid the hills. The pale young leaves of the aspen rustled faintly, not yet with their full sound; the sprays of the horse-chestnut, drooping with the late frosts, could not yet keep out the sunshine with their broad green. A white spot on the footpath yonder was where the bloom had fallen from a blackthorn bush.

The note of the tree-pipit came from over the corn — there were some detached oaks away in the midst of the field, and the birds were doubtless flying continually up and down between the wheat and the branches. A willow-wren sang plaintively in the plantation behind, and once a cuckoo called at a distance. How beautiful is the sunshine! The very dust of the road at my feet seemed to glow with whiteness, to be lit up by it, and to become another thing. This spot henceforward was a place of pilgrimage.

Looking that morning over the parapet of the bridge, down stream, there was a dead branch at the mouth of the arch, it had caught and got fixed while it floated along. A quantity of aquatic weeds coming down the stream had drifted against the branch and remained entangled in it. Fresh weeds were still coming and adding to the mass, which had attracted a water-rat.

Perched on the branch the little brown creature bent forward over the surface, and with its two forepaws drew towards it the slender thread of a weed, exactly as with hands. Holding the thread in the paws, it nibbled it, eating the sweet and tender portion, feeding without fear, though but a few feet away, and precisely beneath me.

In a minute the surface of the current was disturbed by larger ripples. There had been a ripple caused by the draught through the arch, but this was now increased. Directly afterwards a moorhen swam out, and began to search among the edge of the tangled weeds. So long as I was perfectly still the bird took no heed, but at a slight movement instantly scuttled back under the arch. The water-rat, less timorous, paused, looked round, and returned to feeding.

Crossing to the other side of the bridge, up stream, and looking over, the current had scooped away the sand of the bottom by the central pier, exposing the brickwork to some depth — the same undermining process that goes on by the piers of bridges over great rivers. Nearer the shore the sand has silted up, leaving it shallow, where water-parsnip and other weeds joined, as it were, the verge of the grass and the stream. The sunshine reflected from the ripples on this, the southern side, continually ran with a swift, trembling motion up the arch.

Penetrating the clear water, the light revealed the tiniest stone at the bottom: but there was no fish, no water-rat, or moorhen on this side. Neither on that nor many succeeding mornings could anything be seen there; the tail of the arch was evidently the favourite spot. Carefully looking over that side again, the moorhen who had been out rushed back; the water-rat was gone. Were there any fish? In the shadow the water was difficult to see through, and the brown scum of spring that lined the bottom rendered everything uncertain.

By gazing steadily at a stone my eyes presently became accustomed to the peculiar light, the pupils adjusted themselves to it, and the brown tints became more distinctly defined. Then sweeping by degrees from a stone to another, and from thence to a rotting stick embedded in the sand, I searched the bottom inch by inch. If you look, as it were, at large — at everything at once — you see nothing. If you take some object as a fixed point, gaze all around it, and then move to another, nothing can escape.

Even the deepest, darkest water (not, of course, muddy) yields after a while to the eye. Half close the eyelids, and while gazing into it let your intelligence rather wait upon the corners of the eye than on the glance you cast straight forward. For some reason when thus gazing the edge of the eye becomes exceedingly sensitive, and you are conscious of slight motions or of a thickness — not a defined object, but a thickness which indicates an object — which is otherwise quite invisible.

The slow feeling sway of a fish's tail, the edges of which curl over and grasp the water, may in this manner be identified without being positively seen, and the dark outline of its body known to exist against the equally dark water or bank. Shift, too, your position according to the fall of the light, just as in looking at a painting. From one point of view the canvas shows little but the presence of paint and blurred colour, from another at the side the picture stands out.

Sometimes the water can be seen into best from above, sometimes by lying on the sward, now by standing back a little way, or crossing to the opposite shore. A spot where the sunshine sparkles with dazzling gleam is perhaps perfectly impenetrable till you get the other side of the ripple, when the same rays that just now baffled the glance light up the bottom as if thrown from a mirror for the purpose. I convinced myself that there was nothing here, nothing visible at present — not so much as a stickleback.

Yet the stream ran clear and sweet, and deep in places. It was too broad for leaping over. Down the current sedges grew thickly at a curve; up the stream the young flags were rising; it had an inhabited look, if such a term may be used, and moorhens and water-rats were about but no fish. A wide furrow came along the meadow and joined the stream from the side. Into this furrow, at flood time, the stream overflowed further up, and irrigated the level sward.

At present it was dry, its course, traced by the yellowish and white hue of the grasses in it only recently under water, contrasting with the brilliant green of the sweet turf around. There was a marsh marigold in it, with stems a quarter of an inch thick; and in the grass on the verge, but just beyond where the flood reached, grew the lilac-tinted cuckoo flowers, or cardamine.

The side hatch supplied a pond which was only divided from the brook by a strip of sward not more than twenty yards across. The surface of the pond was dotted with patches of scum that had risen from the bottom. Part at least of it was shallow, for a dead branch blown from an elm projected above the water, and to it came a sedge-reedling for a moment. The sedge-reedling is so fond of sedges, and reeds, and thick undergrowth, that though you hear it perpetually within a few yards it is not easy to see one. On this bare branch the bird was well displayed, and the streak by the eye was visible; but he stayed there for a second or two only, and then back again to the sedges and willows.

There were fish I felt sure as I left the spot and returned along the dusty road, but where were they?

A Brook

On the sward by the wayside, among the nettles and under the bushes, and on the mound the dark green arum leaves grew everywhere, sometimes in bunches close together. These bunches varied — in one place the leaves were all spotted with black irregular blotches; in another the leaves were without such markings. When the root leaves of the arum first push up they are closely rolled together in a pointed spike.

This, rising among the dead and matted leaves of the autumn, occasionally passes through holes in them. As the spike grows it lifts the dead leaves with it, which hold it like a ring and prevent it from unfolding. The force of growth is not sufficiently strong to burst the bond asunder till the green leaves have attained considerable size.

A little earlier in the year the chattering of magpies would have been heard while looking for the signs of spring, but they were now occupied with their nests. There are several within a short distance, easily distinguished in winter, but somewhat hidden now by the young leaves. Just before they settled down to housekeeping there was a great chattering and fluttering and excitement, as they chased each other from elm to elm.

Four or five were then often in the same field, some in the trees, some on the ground, their white and black showing distinctly on the level brown earth recently harrowed or rolled. On such a surface birds are visible at a distance; but when the blades of the corn begin to reach any height such as alight are concealed. In many districts of the country that might be called wild and lonely, the magpie is almost extinct. Once now and then a pair may be observed, and those who know their haunts can, of course, find them, but to a visitor passing through, there seems none. But here, so near the metropolis, the magpies are common, and during an hour's walk their cry is almost sure to be heard. They have, however, their favourite locality, where they are much more frequently seen.

Coming to my seat under the aspen by the bridge week after week, the burdocks by the wayside gradually spread their leaves, and the procession of the flowers went on. The dandelion, the lesser celandine, the marsh marigold, the coltsfoot, all yellow, had already led the van, closely accompanied by the purple ground-ivy, the red dead nettle, and the daisy; this last a late comer in the neighbourhood. The blackthorn, the horse-chestnut, and the hawthorn came, and the meadows were golden with the buttercups.

Once only had I noticed any indication of fish in the brook; it was on a warm Saturday afternoon, when there was a labourer a long way up the stream, stooping in a peculiar manner near the edge of the water with a stick in his hand. He was, I felt sure, trying to wire a spawning jack, but did not succeed. Many weeks had passed, and now there came (as the close time for coarse fish expired) a concourse of anglers to the almost stagnant pond fed by the side hatch.

Well-dressed lads with elegant and finished tackle rode up on their bicycles, with their rods slung at their backs. Hoisting the bicycles over the gate into the meadow, they left them leaning against the elms, fitted their rods and fished in the pond. Poorer boys, with long wands cut from the hedge and ruder lines, trudged up on foot, sat down on the sward and watched their corks by the hour together. Grown men of the artisan class, covered with the dust of many miles tramping, came with their luncheons in a handkerchief, and set about their sport with a quiet earnestness which argued long if desultory practise.

In fine weather there were often a dozen youths and four

or five men standing, sitting, or kneeling on the turf along the shore of the pond, all intent on their floats, and very nearly silent. People driving along the highway stopped their traps, and carts, and vans a minute or two to watch them: passengers on foot leaned over the gate, or sat down and waited expectantly.

Sometimes one of the more venturesome anglers would tuck up his trousers and walk into the shallow water, so as to be able to cast his bait under the opposite bank, where it was deep. Then an ancient and much battered punt was discovered aground in a field at some distance, and dragged to the pond. One end of the punt had quite rotted away, but by standing at the other, so as to depress it there and lift the open end above the surface, two, or even three, could make a shift to fish from it.

The silent and motionless eagerness with which these anglers dwelt upon their floats, grave as herons, could not have been exceeded. There they were day after day, always patient and always hopeful. Occasionally a small catch — a mere "bait" — was handed round for inspection; and once a cunning fisherman, acquainted with all the secrets of his craft, succeeded in drawing forth three perch, perhaps a quarter of a pound each, and one slender eel. These made quite a show, and were greatly admired; but I never saw the same man there again. He was satisfied.

As I sat on the white rail under the aspen, and inhaled the scent of the beans flowering hard by, there was a question which suggested itself to me, and the answer to which I never could supply. The crowd about the pond all stood with their backs to the beautiful flowing brook. They had before them the muddy banks of the stagnant pool, on whose surface patches of scum floated.

Behind them was the delicious stream, clear and limpid,

bordered with sedge and willow and flags, and overhung with branches. The strip of sward between the two waters was certainly not more than twenty yards; there was no division, hedge, or railing, and evidently no preservation, for the mouchers came and washed their water-cress which they had gathered in the ditches by the side hatch, and no one interfered with them.

There was no keeper or water bailiff, not even a notice board. Policemen, on foot and mounted, passed several times daily, and, like everybody else, paused to see the sport, but said not a word. Clearly, there was nothing whatever to prevent any of those present from angling in the stream; yet they one and all, without exception, fished in the pond. This seemed to me a very remarkable fact.

After a while I noticed another circumstance; nobody ever even looked into the stream or under the arches of the bridge. No one spared a moment from his float amid the scum of the pond, just to stroll twenty paces and glance at the swift current. It appeared from this that the pond had a reputation for fish, and the brook had not. Everybody who had angled in the pond recommended his friends to go and do likewise. There were fish in the pond.

So every fresh comer went and angled there, and accepted the fact that there were fish. Thus the pond obtained a traditionary reputation, which circulated from lip to lip round about. I need not enlarge on the analogy that exists in this respect between the pond and various other things.

By implication it was evidently as much understood and accepted on the other hand that there was nothing in the stream. Thus I reasoned it out, sitting under the aspen, and yet somehow the general opinion did not satisfy me.

There must be something in so sweet a stream. The sedges by the shore, the flags in the shallow, slowly swaying from side to side with the current, the sedge-reedlings calling, the moorhens and water-rats, all gave an air of habitation.

One morning, looking very gently over the parapet of the bridge (down stream) into the shadowy depth beneath, just as my eyes began to see the bottom, something like a short thick dark stick drifted out from the arch, somewhat sideways. Instead of proceeding with the current, it had hardly cleared the arch when it took a position parallel to the flowing water and brought up. It was thickest at the end that faced the stream; at the other there was a slight motion as if caused by the current against a flexible membrane, as it sways a flag. Gazing down intently into the shadow the colour of the sides of the fish appeared at first not exactly uniform, and presently these indistinct differences resolved themselves into spots. It was a trout, perhaps a pound and a half in weight.

His position was at the side of the arch, out of the rush of the current, and almost behind the pier, but where he could see anything that came floating along under the culvert. Immediately above him but not over was the mass of weeds tangled in the dead branch. Thus in the shadow of the bridge and in the darkness under the weeds he might easily have escaped notice. He was, too, extremely wary. The slightest motion was enough to send him instantly under the arch; his cover was but a foot distant, and a trout shoots twelve inches in a fraction of time.

The summer advanced, the hay was carted, and the wheat ripened. Already here and there the reapers had cut portions of the more forward corn. As I sat from time to time under the aspen, within hearing of the murmuring water, the thought did rise occasionally that it was a pity to leave the trout there till someone blundered into the knowledge of his existence.

There were ways and means by which he could be withdrawn without any noise or publicity. But, then, what would be the pleasure of securing him, the fleeting pleasure of an hour, compared to the delight of seeing him almost day by day? I watched him for many weeks, taking great precautions that no one should observe how continually I looked over into the water there. Sometimes after a glance I stood with my back to the wall as if regarding an object on the other side. If anyone was following me, or appeared likely to peer over the parapet, I carelessly struck the top of the wall with my stick in such a manner that it should project, an action sufficient to send the fish under the arch. Or I raised my hat as if heated, and swung it so that it should alarm him.

If the coast was clear when I had looked at him still I never left without sending him under the arch in order to increase his alertness. It was a relief to know that so many persons who went by wore tall hats, a safeguard against their seeing anything, for if they approached the shadow of the tall hat reached out beyond the shadow of the parapet, and was enough to alarm him before they could look over. So the summer passed, and, though never free from apprehensions, to my great pleasure without discovery.

A London Trout

The sword-flags are rusting at their edges, and their sharp points are turned. On the matted and entangled sedges lie the scattered leaves which every rush of the October wind hurries from the boughs. Some fall on the water and float slowly with the current, brown and yellow spots on the dark surface. The grey willows bend to the breeze; soon the osier beds will look reddish as the wands are stripped by the gusts. Alone the thick polled alders remain green, and in their shadow the brook is still darker. Through a poplar's thin branches the wind sounds as in the rigging of a ship; for the rest, it is silence.

The thrushes have not forgotten the frost of the morning, and will not sing at noon; the summer visitors have flown, and the moorhens feed quietly. The plantation by the brook is silent, for the sedges, though they have drooped and become entangled, are not dry and sapless yet to rustle loudly. They will rustle dry enough next spring, when the sedge-birds come. A long withey-bed borders the brook, and is more resorted to by sedge-reedlings, or sedge-birds, as they are variously called, than any place I know, even in the remotest country.

Generally it has been difficult to see them, because the withey is in leaf when they come, and the leaves and sheaves of innumerable rods hide them, while the ground beneath is covered by a thick growth of sedges and flags, to which the birds descend. It happened once, however, that the withey stoles had been polled, and in the spring the boughs were short and small. At the same time, the easterly winds checked the sedges, so that they were hardly half their height, and the flags were thin, and not much taller, when the sedge-birds came, so that they for once found but little cover, and could be seen to advantage.

There could not have been less than fifteen in the plantation, two frequented some bushes beside a pond near by, some stayed in scattered willows farther down the stream. They sang so much they scarcely seemed to have time to feed. While approaching one that was singing by gently walking on the sward by the road-side, or where thick dust deadened the footsteps, suddenly another would commence in the low thorn hedge on a branch, so near that it could be touched with a walking stick. Yet though so near the bird was not wholly visible — he was partly concealed behind a fork of the bough. This is a habit of the sedge-birds. Not in the least timid, they chatter at your elbow, and yet always partially hidden.

If in the withey, they choose a spot where the rods cross or bunch together. If in the sedges, though so close it seems as if you could reach forward and catch him, he is behind the stalks. To place some obstruction between themselves and anyone passing is their custom; but that spring, as the foliage was so thin, it only needed a little dexterity in peering to get a view. The sedge-bird perches aside, on a sloping willow rod, and, slightly raising his head, chatters, turning his bill from side to side. He is a very tiny bird, and his little eye looks out from under a yellowish streak. His song at first sounds nothing but chatter.

After listening a while the ear finds a scale in it — an arrangement and composition — so that, though still a chatter, it is a tasteful one. At intervals he intersperses a chirp, exactly the same as that of the sparrow, a chirp with a tang in it. Strike a piece of metal, and besides the noise of the blow, there is a second note, or tang. The sparrow's chirp has such a note sometimes, and the sedge-bird brings it in — tang, tang, tang. This sound has given him his country name of brook-sparrow, and it rather spoils his song. Often the moment he has concluded he starts for another willow stole, and as he flies begins to chatter when half way across, and finishes on a fresh branch.

But long before this another bird has commenced to sing in a bush adjacent; a third takes it up in the thorn hedge; a fourth in the bushes across the pond; and from farther down the stream comes a faint and distant chatter. Ceaselessly the competing gossip goes on the entire day and most of the night; indeed sometimes all night through. On a warm spring morning, when the sunshine pours upon the willows, and even the white dust of the road is brighter, bringing out the shadows in clear definition, their lively notes and quick motions make a pleasant commentary on the low sound of the stream rolling round the curve.

A moorhen's call comes from the hatch. Broad yellow

petals of marsh-marigold stand up high among the sedges rising from the greyish-green ground, which is covered with a film of sun-dried aquatic grass left dry by the retiring waters. Here and there are lilac-tinted cuckoo-flowers, drawn up on taller stalks than those that grow in the meadows. The black flowers of the sedges are powdered with yellow pollen; and dark green sword-flags are beginning to spread their fans. But just across the road, on the topmost twigs of birch poles, swallows twitter in the tenderest tones to their loves. From the oaks in the meadows on that side titlarks mount above the highest bough and then descend, sing, sing, singing, to the grass.

A jay calls in a circular copse in the midst of the meadow; solitary rooks go over to their nests in the elms on the hill; cuckoos call, now this way and now that, as they travel round. While leaning on the grey and lichen-hung rails by the brook, the current glides by, and it is the motion of the water and its low murmur which renders the place so idle; the sunbeams brood, the air is still but full of song. Let us, too, stay and watch the petals fall one by one from a wild apple and float down on the stream.

But now in autumn the haws are red on the thorn, the swallows are few as they were in the earliest spring; the sedge-birds have flown, and the redwings will soon be here. The sharp points of the sword-flags are turned, their edges rusty, the forget-me-nots are gone. October's winds are too searching for us to linger beside the brook, but still it is pleasant to pass by and remember the summer days. For the year is never gone by; in a moment we can recall the sunshine we enjoyed in May, the roses we gathered in June, the first wheat-ear we plucked as the green corn filled. Other events go by and are forgotten, and even the details of our own lives, so immensely important to us at the moment, in time fade from the memory till the date we fancied we should never forget has to be sought in a diary. But the year is always with us; the months are familiar always; they have never gone by.

So with the red haws around and the rustling leaves it is easy to recall the flowers. The withey plantation here is full of flowers in summer; yellow iris flowers in June when midsummer comes, for the iris loves a thunder-shower. The flowering flag spreads like a fan from the root, the edges overlap near the ground, and the leaves are broad as sword-blades, indeed the plant is one of the largest that grows wild. It is quite different from the common flag with three groves — bayonet shape — which appears in every brook. The yellow iris is much more local, and in many country streams may be sought for in vain, so that so fine a display as may be seen here seemed almost a discovery to me.

They were finest in the year of rain, 1879, that terrible year which is fresh in the memory of all who have any interest in out-of-door matters. At mid-summer the plantation was aglow with iris bloom. The large yellow petals were everywhere high above the sedge; in one place a dozen, then two or three, then one by itself, then another bunch. The marsh was a foot deep in water, which could only be seen by parting the stalks of the sedges, for it was quite hidden under them. Sedges and flags grew so thick that everything was concealed except the yellow bloom above.

One bunch grew on a bank raised a few inches above the flood which the swollen brook had poured in, and there I walked among them; the leaves came nearly up to the shoulder, the golden flowers on the stalks stood equally high. It was a thicket of iris. Never before had they risen to such a height; it was like the vegetation of tropical swamps, so much was everything drawn up by the continual moisture. Who could have supposed that such a downpour as occurred that summer would have had the effect it had upon flowers? Most would have imagined that the excessive rain would have destroyed them; yet never was there such floral beauty as that year. Meadow orchis, buttercups, the yellow iris, all the spring flowers came forth in extraordinary profusion. The hay was spoiled, the farmers ruined, but their fields were one broad expanse of flower.

As that spring was one of the wettest, so that of the year in present view was one of the driest, and hence the plantation between the lane and the brook was accessible, the sedges and flags short, and the sedge-birds visible. There is a beech in the plantation standing so near the verge of the stream that its boughs droop over. It has a number of twigs around the stem — as a rule the beechbole is clear of boughs, but some which are of rather stunted growth are fringed with them. The leaves on the longer boughs above fall off and voyage down the brook, but those on the lesser twigs beneath, and only a little way from the ground, remain on, and rustle, dry and brown, all through the winter.

Under the shelter of these leaves, and close to the trunk, there grew a plant of flag — the tops of the flags almost reached to the leaves — and all the winter through, despite the frosts for which it was remarkable, despite the snow and the bitter winds which followed, this plant remained green and fresh. From this beech in the morning a shadow stretches to a bridge across the brook, and in that shadow my trout used to lie. The bank under the drooping boughs forms a tiny cliff a foot high, covered with moss, and here

CHOLERTON 82

I once observed shrew mice diving and racing about. But only once, though I frequently passed the spot; it is curious that I did not see them afterwards.

Just below the shadow of the beech there is a sandy oozy shore, where the footprints of moorhens are often traceable. Many of the trees of the plantation stand in water after heavy rain; their leaves drop into it in autumn, and, being away from the influence of the current, stay and soak, and lie several layers thick. Their edges overlap, red, brown, and pale yellow, with the clear water above and shadows athwart it, and dry white grass at the verge. A horse-chestnut drops its fruit in the dusty road; high above its leaves are tinted with scarlet.

It was at the tail of one of the arches of the bridge over the brook that my favourite trout used to lie. Sometimes the shadow of the beech came as far as his haunts, that was early in the morning, and for the rest of the day the bridge itself cast a shadow. The other parapet faces the south, and looking down from it the bottom of the brook is generally visible, because the light is so strong. At the bottom a green plant may be seen waving to and fro in summer as the current sways it. It is not a weed or flag, but a plant with pale green leaves, and looks as if it had come there by some chance; this is the water-parsnip.

By the shore on this, the sunny side of the bridge, a few forget-me-nots grow in their season, water crow's-foot flowers, flags lie along the surface and slowly swing from side to side like a boat at anchor. The breeze brings a ripple, and the sunlight sparkles on it; the light reflected dances up the piers of the bridge. Those that pass along the road are naturally drawn to this bright parapet where the brook winds brimming full through green meadows. You can see right to the bottom; you can see where the rush of the water has scooped out a deeper channel under the arches, but look as long as you like there are no fish.

The trout I watched so long, and with such pleasure, was always on the other side, at the tail of the arch, waiting for whatever might come through to him. There in perpetual shadow he lay in wait, a little at the side of the arch, scarcely ever varying his position except to dart a yard up under the bridge to seize anything he fancied, and drifting out again to bring up at his anchorage. If people looked over the parapet that side they did not see him; they could not see the bottom there for the shadow, or if the summer noonday cast a strong beam even then it seemed to cover the surface of the water with a film of light which could not be seen through. There are some aspects from which even a picture hung on the wall close at hand cannot be seen. So no one saw the trout; if anyone more curious leant over the parapet he was gone in a moment under the arch.

Folk fished in the pond about the verge of which the sedge-birds chattered, and but a few yards distant; but they never looked under the arch on the northern and shadowy side, where the water flowed beside the beech. For three seasons this continued. For three summers I had the pleasure to see the trout day after day whenever I walked that way, and all that time, with fishermen close at hand, he escaped notice, though the place was not preserved. It is wonderful to think how difficult it is to see anything under one's very eyes, and thousands of people walked actually and physically right over the fish.

However, one morning in the third summer, I found a fisherman standing in the road and fishing over the parapet in the shadowy water. But he was fishing at the wrong arch, and only with paste for roach. While the man stood there fishing, along came two navvies; naturally enough they went quietly up to see what the fisherman was doing, and one instantly uttered an exclamation. He had seen the trout. The man who was fishing with paste had stood so still and patient that the trout, re-assured, had come out, and the navvy — trust a navvy to see anything of the kind — caught sight of him.

The navvy knew how to see through water. He told the fisherman, and there was a stir of excitement, a changing of hooks and bait. I could not stay to see the result, but went on, fearing the worst. But he did not succeed; next day the wary trout was there still, and the next, and the next. Either this particular fisherman was not able to come again, or was discouraged; at any rate, he did not try again. The fish escaped, doubtless more wary than ever.

In the spring of the next year the trout was still there, and up to the summer I used to go and glance at him. This was the fourth season, and still he was there; I took friends to look at this wonderful fish, which defied all the loafers and poachers, and above all, surrounded himself not only with the shadow of the bridge, but threw a mental shadow over the minds of passers-by, so that they never thought of the possibility of such a thing as trout. But one morning something happened. The brook was dammed up on the sunny side of the bridge, and the water let off by a side-hatch, that some accursed main or pipe or other horror might be laid across the bed of the stream somewhere far down.

Above the bridge there was a brimming broad brook, below it the flags lay on the mud, the weeds drooped, and the channel was dry. It was dry up to the beech tree. There, under the drooping boughs of the beech, was a small pool of muddy water, perhaps two yards long, and very narrow

—a stagnant muddy pool, not more than three or four inches deep. In this I saw the trout. In the shallow water, his back came up to the surface (for his fins must have touched the mud sometimes) — once it came above the surface, and his spots showed as plain as if you had held him in your hand. He was swimming round to try and find out the reason of this sudden stinting of room.

Twice he heaved himself somewhat on his side over a dead branch that was at the bottom, and exhibited all his beauty to the air and sunshine. Then he went away into another part of the shallow and was hidden by the muddy water. Now under the arch of the bridge, his favourite arch, close by there was a deep pool, for, as already mentioned, the scour of the current scooped away the sand and made a hole there. When the stream was shut off by the dam above this hole remained partly full. Between this pool and the shallow under the beech there was sufficient connection for the fish to move into it.

My only hope was that he would do so, and as some showers fell, temporarily increasing the depth of the narrow canal between the two pools, there seemed every reason to believe that he had got to that under the arch. If now only that accursed pipe or main, or whatever repair it was, could only be finished quickly, even now the trout might escape! Every day my anxiety increased, for the intelligence would soon get about that the brook was dammed up, and any pools left in it would be sure to attract attention.

Sunday came, and directly the bells had done ringing four men attacked the pool under the arch. They took off shoes and stockings and waded in, two at each end of the arch. Stuck in the mud close by was an eel-spear. They churned up the mud, wading in, and thickened and darkened it as they groped under. No one could watch these barbarians longer.

Is it possible that he could have escaped? He was a wonderful fish, wary and quick. Is it just possible that they may not even have known that a trout was there at all; but have merely hoped for perch, or tench, or eels? The pool was deep and the fish quick — they did not bale it, might he have escaped? Might they even, if they did find him, have mercifully taken him and placed him alive in some other water nearer their homes? Is it possible that he may have almost miraculously made his way down the stream into other pools?

There was very heavy rain one night, which might have given him such a chance. These "mights," and "ifs," and "is it possible" even now keep alive some little hope that some day I may yet see him again. But that was early in the summer. It is now winter, and the beech has brown spots. Among the limes the sedges are matted and entangled, the sword-flags rusty; the rooks are at the acorns, and the plough is at work in the stubble. I have never seen him since. I never failed to glance over the parapet into the shadowy water. Somehow it seemed to look colder, darker, less pleasant than it used to do. The spot was empty, and the shrill winds whistled through the poplars.

Wild Flowers

A FIR-TREE is not a flower, and yet it is associated in my mind with primroses. There was a narrow lane leading into a wood, where I used to go almost every day in the early months of the year, and at one corner it was overlooked by three spruce firs. The rugged lane there began to ascend the hill, and I paused a moment to look back. Immediately the high fir-trees guided the eye upwards, and from their tops to the deep azure of the March sky over, but a step from the tree to the heavens. So it has ever been to me, by day or by night, summer or winter, beneath trees the heart feels nearer to that depth of life the far sky means. The rest of spirit found only in beauty, ideal and pure, comes there because the distance seems within touch of thought. To the heaven thought can reach lifted by the strong arms of the oak, carried up by the ascent of the flame-shaped fir. Round the spruce top the blue was deepened, concentrated by the fixed point; the memory of that spot, as it were, of the sky is still fresh — I can see it distinctly — still beautiful and full of meaning. It is painted in bright colour in my mind, colour thrice laid, and indelible; as one passes a shrine and bows the head to the Madonna, so I recall the picture and stoop in spirit to the aspiration it yet arouses. For there is no saint like the sky, sunlight shining from its face.

The fir-tree flowered thus before the primroses — the first of all to give me a bloom, beyond reach but visible, while even the hawthorn buds hesitated to open. Primroses were late there, a high district and thin soil; you could read of them as found elsewhere in January; they rarely came much before March, and but sparingly then. On the warm red sand (red, at least, to look at, but green by geological courtesy, I think) of Sussex, round about Hurst of the Pierrepoints, primroses are seen soon after the year has turned. In the lanes about that curious old mansion, with its windows reaching from floor to roof, that stands at the base of Wolstanbury Hill, they grow early, and ferns linger in sheltered overhung banks. The South Down range, like a great wall, shuts off the sea, and has a different climate on either hand; south by the sea — hard, harsh, flowerless, almost grassless, bitter, and cold; on the north side, just over the hill — warm, soft, with primroses and fern, willows budding and birds already busy. It is a double England there, two countries side by side.

On a summer's day Wolstanbury Hill is an island in sunshine; you may lie on the grassy rampart, high up in the most delicate air — Grecian air, pellucid — alone, among the butterflies and humming bees at the thyme, alone and isolated; endless masses of hills on three sides, endless weald or valley on the fourth; all warmly lit with sunshine, deep under liquid sunshine like the sands under the liquid sea, no harshness of man-made sound to break the insulation amid nature, on an island in a far Pacific of sunshine. Some people would hesitate to walk down the staircase cut in the turf to the beech trees beneath; the woods look so small beneath, so far down and steep, and no handrail. Many go to the Dyke, but none to Wolstanbury Hill. To come over the range reminds one of what travellers say of coming over the Alps into Italy; from harsh sea-slopes, made dry with salt as they sow salt on razed cities that naught may grow, to warm plains rich in all things, and with great hills as pictures hung on a wall to gaze at. Where there are beech trees the land is always beautiful; beech trees at the foot of this hill, beech trees at Arundel in that lovely park which the Duke of Norfolk, to his glory, leaves open to all the world, and where the anenomes flourish in unusual size and number; beech trees in Marlborough Forest; beech trees at the summit to which the lane leads that was spoken of just now. Beech and beautiful scenery go together.

But the primroses by that lane did not appear till late; they covered the banks under the thousand thousand ash-poles, foxes slipped along there frequently, whose friends in scarlet coats could not endure the pale flowers, for they might chink their spurs homewards. In one meadow near primroses were thicker than the grass, with gorse interspersed, and the rabbits that came out fed among flowers. The primroses last on to the celandines and cowslips, through the time of the bluebells, past the violets — one dies but passes on the life to another, one sets light to the next, till the ruddy oaks and singing cuckoos call up the tall mowing-grass to fringe summer.

Before I had any conscious thought it was a delight to me to find wild flowers, just to see them. It was a pleasure to gather them and to take them home; a pleasure to show them to others — to keep them as long as they would live, to decorate the room with them, to arrange them carelessly with grasses, green sprays, tree-bloom — large branches of chestnut snapped off, and set by a picture perhaps. Without conscious thought of seasons and the advancing hours to light on the white wild violet, the meadow orchis, the blue veronica, the blue meadow cranesbill; feeling the warmth and delight of the increasing sun-rays, but not recognizing whence or why it was joy. All the world is young to a boy, and thought has not entered into it; even the old men with grey hair do not seem old; different but not aged, the idea of age has not been mastered. A boy has to frown and study, and then does not grasp what long years mean. The various hues of the petals pleased without any knowledge of colour-contrasts, no note even of colour except that it was bright, and the mind was made happy without consideration of those ideals and hopes afterwards associated with the azure sky above the fir tree. A fresh footpath, a fresh flower, a fresh delight. The reeds, the grasses, the rushes — unknown and new things at every step — something always to find; no barren spot anywhere, or sameness. Every day the grass painted anew, and its green seen for the first time; not the old green, but a novel hue and spectacle, like the first view of the sea.

If we had never before looked upon the earth, but suddenly came to it man or woman grown, set down in the midst of a summer mead, would it not seem to us a radiant vision? The hues, the shapes, the song and life of birds, above all the sunlight, the breath of heaven, resting on it; the mind would be filled with its glory, unable to grasp it, hardly believing that such things could be mere matter and no more. Like a dream of some spirit-land it would appear, scarce fit to be touched lest it should fall to pieces, too beautiful to be long watched lest it should fade away. So it seemed to me as a boy, sweet and new like this each morning; and even now, after the years that have passed, and the lines they have worn in the forehead, the summer mead shines as bright and fresh as when my foot first touched the grass. It has another meaning now; the sunshine and the flowers speak differently, for a heart that has once known sorrow reads behind the page, and sees sadness in joy. But the freshness is still there, the dew washes the colours before dawn. Unconscious happiness in finding wild flowers — unconscious and unquestioning, and therefore unbounded.

I used to stand by the mower and follow the scythe sweeping down thousands of the broad-flowered daisies, the knotted knapweeds, the blue scabious, the yellow rattles, sweeping so close and true that nothing escaped; and yet, although I had seen so many hundreds of each, although I had lifted armfuls day after day, still they were fresh. They never lost their newness, and even now each time I gather a wild flower it feels a new thing. The greenfinches came to the fallen swathe so near to us they seemed to have no fear; but I remember the yellowhammers most, whose colour, like that of the wild flowers and the sky, has never faded from my memory. The greenfinches sank into the fallen swathe, the loose grass gave under their weight and let them bathe in flowers.

One yellowhammer sat on a branch of ash the livelong morning, still singing in the sun; his bright head, his clean bright yellow, gaudy as Spain, was drawn like a brush charged heavily with colour across the retina, painting it deeply, for there on the eye's memory it endures, though that was boyhood and this is manhood, still unchanged. The field — Stewart's Mash — the very tree, young ash timber, the branch projecting over the sward, I could make a map of them. Sometimes I think sun-painted colours are brighter to me than to many, and more strongly affect the nerves of the eye. Straw going by the road on a dusky winter's day seems so pleasantly golden, the sheaves lying aslant at the top, and these bundles of yellow tubes thrown up against the dark ivy on the opposite wall. Tiles, red burned, or orange coated, the sea sometimes cleanly definite, the shadows of trees in a thin wood where there is room for shadows to form and fall; some such shadows are sharper than light, and have a faint blue tint. Not only in summer but in cold winter, and not only romantic things but plain matter-of-fact things, as a waggon freshly painted red beside the wright's shop, stand out as if wet with colour and delicately pencilled at the edges. It must be out of doors; nothing indoors looks like this.

Pictures are very dull and gloomy to it, and very contrasted colours like those the French use are necessary to fix the attention. Their dashes of pink and scarlet bring the faint shadow of the sun into the room. As for our painters, their works are hung behind a curtain, and we have to peer patiently through the dusk of evening to see what they mean. Out-of-door colours do not need to be gaudy — a mere dull stake of wood thrust in the ground often stands out sharper than the pink flashes of the French studio; a faggot; the outline of a leaf; low tints without reflecting power strike the eye as a bell the ear. To me

CHOLERTON '82

they are intensely clear, and the clearer the greater the pleasure. It is often too great, for it takes me away from solid pursuits merely to receive the impression, as water is still to reflect the trees. To me it is very painful when illness blots the definition of outdoor things, so wearisome not to see them rightly, and more oppressive than actual pain. I feel as if I was struggling to wake up with dim, half-opened lids and heavy mind. This one yellowhammer still sits on the ash branch in Stewart's Mash over the sward, singing in the sun, his feathers freshly wet with colour, the same sun-song, and will sing to me so long as the heart shall beat.

The first conscious thought about wild flowers was to find out their names — the first conscious pleasure — and then I began to see so many that I had not previously noticed. Once you wish to identify them there is nothing escapes, down to the little white chickweed of the path and the moss of the wall. I put my hand on the bridge across the brook to lean over and look down into the water. Are there any fish? The bricks of the pier are covered with green, like a wall-painting to the surface of the stream, mosses along the lines of the mortar, and among the moss little plants — what are these? In the dry sunlit lane I look up to the top of the great wall about some domain, where the green figs look over upright on their stalks; there are dry plants on the coping — what are these? Some growing thus, high in the air, on stone, and in the chinks of the tower, suspended in dry air and sunshine; some low down under the arch of the bridge over the brook, out of sight utterly, unless you stoop by the brink of the water and project yourself forward to examine under. The kingfisher sees them as he shoots through the barrel of the culvert. There the sun direct never shines upon them, but the sunlight thrown up by the ripples runs all day in bright bars along the vault of the arch, playing on them. The stream arranges the sand in the shallow in bars, minute fixed undulations; the stream arranges the sunshine in successive flashes, undulating as if the sun, drowsy in the heat, were idly closing and unclosing his eyelids for sleep. Plants everywhere, hiding behind every tree, under the leaves, in the shady places, beside the dry furrows of the field; they are only just behind something, hidden openly. The instant you look for them they multiply a hundred-fold; if you sit on the beach and begin to count the pebbles by you, their number instantly increases to infinity by virtue of that conscious act.

The bird's-foot lotus was the first. The boy must have seen it, must have trodden on it in the bare woodland pastures, certainly run about on it, with wet naked feet from the bathing; but the boy was not conscious of it. This was the first, when the desire came to identify and to know, fixing upon it by means of a pale and feeble picture. In the largest pasture there were different soils and climates; it was so large it seemed a little country of itself then — the more so because the ground rose and fell, making a ridge to divide the view and enlarge by uncertainty. The high sandy soil on the ridge where the rabbits had their warren; the rocky soil of the quarry; the long grass by the elms where the rooks built, under whose nests there were vast unpalatable mushrooms — the true mushrooms with salmon gills grew nearer the warren; the slope towards the nut-tree hedge and spring. Several climates in one field: the wintry ridge over which leaves were always driving in all four seasons of the year; the level sunny plain and fallen cromlech still tall enough for a gnomon and to cast its shadow in the treeless drought;

the moist, warm, grassy depression; the lotus-grown slope, warm and dry.

If you have been living in one house in the country for some time, and then go on a visit to another, though hardly half a mile distant, you will find a change in the air, the feeling, and tone of the place. It is close by, but it is not the same. To discover these minute differences, which make one locality healthy and home happy, and the next adjoining unhealthy, the Chinese have invented the science of Feng-shui, spying about with cabalistic mystery, casting the horoscope of an acre. There is something in all superstitions; they are often the foundation of science. Superstition having made the discovery, science composes a lecture on the reason why, and claims the credit. Bird's-foot lotus means a fortunate spot, dry, warm — so far as soil is concerned. If you were going to live out of doors, you might safely build your kibitka where you found it. Wandering with the pictured flower-book, just purchased, over the windy ridge where last year's skeleton leaves, blown out from the alder copse below, came on with grasshopper motion — lifted and laid down by the wind, lifted and laid down — I sat on the sward of the sheltered slope, and instantly recognized the orange-red claws of the flower beside me. That was the first; and this very morning, I dread to consider how many years afterwards, I found a plant on a wall which I do not know. I shall have to trace out its genealogy and emblazon its shield. So many years and still only at the beginning — the beginning, too, of the beginning — for as yet I have not thought of the garden or conservatory flowers (which are wild flowers somewhere), or of the tropics, or the prairies.

The great stone of the fallen cromlech, crouching down afar off in the plain behind me, cast its shadow in the sunny morn as it had done, so many summers, for centuries — for thousands of years: worn white by the endless sunbeams — the ceaseless flood of light — the sunbeams of centuries, the impalpable beams polishing and grinding like rushing water: silent, yet witnessing of the Past; shadowing the Present on the dial of the field: a mere dull stone; but what is it the mind will not employ to express to itself its own thoughts?

There was a hollow near in which hundreds of skeleton leaves had settled, a stage on their journey from the alder copse, so thick as to cover the thin grass, and at the side of the hollow a wasp's nest had been torn out by a badger. On the soft and spreading sand thrown out from his burrow the print of his foot looked as large as an elephant might make. The wild animals of our fields are so small that the badger's foot seemed foreign in its size, calling up the thought of the great game of distant forests. He was a bold badger to make his burrow there in the open warren, unprotected by park walls or preserve laws, where every one might see who chose. I never saw him by daylight: that they do get about in daytime is, however, certain, for one was shot in Surrey recently by sportsmen; they say he weighed forty pounds.

In the mind all things are written in pictures — there is no alphabetical combination of letters and words; all things are pictures and symbols. The bird's-foot lotus is the picture to me of sunshine and summer, and of that summer in the heart which is known only in youth, and then not alone. No words could write that feeling: the bird's-foot lotus writes it.

When the efforts to photograph began, the difficulty was to fix the scene thrown by the lens upon the plate. There the view appeared perfect to the least of details, worked out by the sun, and made as complete in miniature as that he shone upon in nature. But it faded like the shadows as the summer sun declines. Have you watched them in the fields among the flowers? — the deep strong mark of the noonday shadow of a tree such as the pen makes drawn heavily on the paper; gradually it loses its darkness and becomes paler and thinner at the edges as it lengthens and spreads, till shadow and grass mingle together. Image after image faded from the plates, no more to be fixed than the reflection in water of the trees by the shore. Memory, like the sun, paints to me bright pictures of the golden summer time of lotus; I can see them, but how shall I fix them for you? By no process can that be accomplished. It is like a story that cannot be told because he who knows it is tongue-tied and dumb. Motions of hands, wavings and gestures, rudely convey the framework, but the finish is not there.

Today, and day after day, fresh pictures are coloured instantaneously in the retina as bright and perfect in detail and hue. This very power is often, I think, the cause of pain to me. To see so clearly is to value so highly and to feel too deeply. The smallest of the pencilled branches of the bare ash tree drawn distinctly against the winter sky, waving lines one within the other, yet following and partly parallel, reproducing in the curve of the twig the curve of the great trunk; is it not a pleasure to trace each to its ending? The raindrops as they slide from leaf to leaf in June, the balmy shower that reperfumes each wild flower and green thing, drops lit with the sun, and falling to the chorus of the refreshed birds; is not this beautiful to see? On the grasses tall and heavy the purplish blue pollen, a shimmering dust, sown broadcast over the ripening meadow from July's warm hand — the bluish pollen, the lilac pollen of the grasses, a delicate mist of blue floating on the surface, has always been an especial delight to me. Finches shake it from the stalks as they rise. No day, no hour of summer, no step but brings new mazes — there is no word to express design without plan, and these designs of flower and leaf and colours of the sun cannot be reduced to set order. The eye is for ever drawn onward and finds no end. To see these always so sharply, wet and fresh, is almost too much sometimes for the wearied yet insatiate eye. I am obliged to turn away — to shut my eyes and say I *will* not see, I will concentrate my mind on my own little path of life, and steadily gaze downwards. In vain. Who can do so? Who can care alone for his or her petty trifles of existence, that has once entered amongst the wild flowers? How shall I shut out the sun? Shall I deny the constellations of the night? They are there; the Mystery is for ever about us — the question, the hope, the aspiration cannot be put out. So that it is almost a pain not to be able to cease observing and tracing the untraceable maze of beauty.

Blue veronica was the next identified, sometimes called germander speedwell, sometimes bird's-eye, whose leaves are so plain and petals so blue. Many names increase the trouble of identification, and confusion is made certain by the use of various systems of classification. The flower itself I knew, its name I could not be sure of — not even from the illustration, which was incorrectly coloured; the central white spot of the flower was reddish in the plate. This incorrect colouring spoils much of the flower-picturing done; pictures of flowers and birds are rarely accurate unless hand-painted. Anyone else, however, would have been quite satisfied that the identification was right. I was too desirous to be correct, too conscientious, and thus a summer went by with little progress. If you really wish to identify with certainty, and have no botanist friend and no *magnum opus* of Sowerby to refer to, it is very difficult indeed to be quite sure. There was no Sowerby, no Bentham, no botanist friend — no one even to give the common country names; for it is a curious fact that the country people of the time rarely know the names put down as the vernacular for flowers in the books.

No one there could tell me the name of the marsh-marigold which grew thickly in the water-meadows — "A sort of big buttercup," that was all they knew. Commonest of common plants is the "sauce alone" — in every hedge, on every bank, the whitish-green leaf is found — yet I could not make certain of it. If someone tells you a plant, you know it at once and never forget it, but to learn it from a book is another matter; it does not at once take root in the mind, it has to be seen several times before you are satisfied — you waver in your convictions. The leaves were described as large and heart-shaped, and to remain green (at the ground) through the winter; but the colour of the flower was omitted, though it was stated that the petals of the hedge-mustard were yellow. The plant that seemed to me to be probably "sauce alone" had leaves somewhat heart-shaped, but so confusing is *partial* description that I began to think I had hit on "ramsons" instead of "sauce alone," especially as ramsons was said to be a very common plant. So it is in some counties, but, as I afterwards found, there was not a plant of ramsons, or garlic, throughout the whole of that district. When, some years afterwards, I saw a white-flowered plant with leaves like the lily of the valley, smelling of garlic, in the woods of Somerset, I recognized it immediately. The plants that are really common — common everywhere —

are not numerous, and if you are studying you must be careful to understand that word locally. My "sauce alone" identification was right; to be right and not certain is still unsatisfactory.

There shone on the banks white stars among the grass. Petals delicately white in a whorl of rays — light that had started radiating from a centre and become fixed — shining among the flowerless green. The slender stem had grown so fast it had drawn its own root partly out of the ground, and when I tried to gather it, flower, stem and root came away together. The wheat was springing, the soft air full of the growth and moisture, blackbirds whistling, wood-pigeons nesting, young oak-leaves out; a sense of swelling, sunny fullness in the atmosphere. The plain road was made beautiful by the advanced boughs that overhung and cast their shadows on the dust — boughs of ash-green, shadows that lay still, listening to the nightingale. A place of enchantment in the mornings, where was felt the power of some subtle influence working behind bough and grass and bird-song. The orange-golden dandelion in the sward was deeply laden with colour brought to it anew again and again by the ships of the flowers, the humble-bees — to their quays they come, unlading priceless essences of sweet odours brought from the East over the green seas of wheat, unlading priceless colours on the broad dandelion discs, bartering these things for honey and pollen. Slowly tacking aslant, the pollen ship hums in the south wind. The little brown wren finds her way through the great thicket of hawthorn. How does she know her path, hidden by a thousand thousand leaves? Tangled and crushed together by their own growth, a crown of thorns hangs over the thrush's nest; thorns for the mother, hope for the young. Is there a crown of thorns over your heart? A spike has gone deep enough into mine. The stile looks farther away because boughs have pushed forward and made it smaller. The willow scarce holds the sap that tightens the bark and would burst it if it did not enlarge to the pressure.

Two things can go through the solid oak; the lightning of the clouds that rends the iron timber, the lightning of the spring — the electricity of the sunbeams forcing him to stretch forth and lengthen his arms with joy. Bathed in buttercups to the dewlap, the roan cows standing in the golden lake watched the hours with calm frontlet; watched the light descending, the meadows filling, with knowledge of long months of succulent clover. On their broad brows the year falls gently; their great, beautiful eyes, which need but a tear or a smile to make them human — without these, such eyes, so large and full, seem above human life, eyes of the immortals enduring without passion, — in these eyes, as a mirror, nature is reflected.

I came every day to walk slowly up and down the plain road, by the starry flowers under the ash-green boughs; ash is the coolest, softest green. The bees went drifting over by my head; as they cleared the hedges they passed by my ears, the wind singing in their shrill wings. White tent-walls of cloud — a warm white, being full to overflowing of sunshine — stretched across from ash-top to ash-top, a cloud-canvas roof, a tent-palace of the delicious air. For of all things there is none so sweet as sweet air — one great flower it is, drawn round about, over, and enclosing, like Aphrodite's arms; as if the dome of the sky were a bell-flower drooping down over us, and the magical essence of it filling all the room of the earth. Sweetest of all things is wild-flower air. Full of their ideal the starry flowers strained upwards on the bank, striving

to keep above the rude grasses that pushed by them; genius has ever had such a struggle. The plain road was made beautiful by the many thoughts it gave. I came every morning to stay by the star-lit bank.

A friend said, "Why do you go the same road every day? Why not have a change and walk somewhere else sometimes? Why keep on up and down the same place?" I could not answer; till then it had not occurred to me that I did always go one way; as for the reason of it I could not tell; I continued in my old mind while the summers went away. Not till years afterwards was I able to see why I went the same round and did not care for change. I do not want to change: I want the same old and loved things, the same wild flowers, the same trees and soft ash-green; the turtle-doves, the blackbirds, the coloured yellow-hammer sing, sing, singing so long as there is light to cast a shadow on the dial, for such is the measure of his song, and I want them in the same place. Let me find them morning after morning, the starry-white petals radiating, striving upwards to their ideal. Let me see the idle shadows resting on the white dust; let me hear the humble-bees, and stay to look down on the rich dandelion disc. Let me see the very thistles opening their great crowns — I should miss the thistles; the reed-grasses hiding the moor-hen; the bryony bine, at first crudely ambitious and lifted by force of youthful sap straight above the hedgerow to sink of its own weight presently and progress with crafty tendrils; swifts shot through the air with out-stretched wings like crescent-headed shaftless arrows darted from the clouds; the chaffinch with a feather in her bill; all the living staircase of the spring, step by step, upwards to the great gallery of the summer — let me watch the same succession year by year.

Why, I knew the very dates of them all — the reddening elm, the arum, the hawthorn leaf, the celandine, the may; the yellow iris of the waters, the heath of the hillside. The time of the nightingale — the place to hear the first note; onwards to the drooping fern and the time of the redwing — the place of *his* first note, so welcome to the sportsman as the acorn ripens and the pheasant, come to the age of manhood, feeds himself; onwards to the shadowless days — the long shadowless winter, for in winter it is the shadows we miss as much as the light. They lie over the summer sward, design upon design, dark lace on green and gold; they glorify the sunlight; they repose on the distant hills like gods upon Olympus; without shadow what even is the sun? At the foot of the great cliffs by the sea you may know this, it is dry glare; mighty ocean is dearer as the shadows of the clouds sweep over as they sweep over the green corn. Past the shadowless winter, when it is all shade, and therefore no shadow; onwards to the first coltsfoot and on to the seedtime again; I knew the dates of all of them. I did not want change; I wanted the same flowers to return on the same day, the titlark to rise soaring from the same oak to fetch down love with a song from heaven to his mate on the nest beneath. No change, no new thing; if I found a fresh wild flower in a fresh place, still it wove at once into the old garland. In vain, the very next year was different even in the same place — *that* had been a year of rain, and the flag flowers were wonderful to see; *this* was a dry year, and the flags not half the height, the gold of the flower not so deep; next year the fatal billhook came and swept away a slow-grown hedge that had given me crab-blossom in cuckoo-time and hazelnuts in harvest. Never again the same, even in the same place.

Wild Flowers

A little feather droops downwards to the ground — a swallow's feather fuller of miracle than the Pentateuch — how shall that feather be placed again in the breast where it grew? Nothing twice. Time changes the places that knew us, and if we go back in after years, still even then it is not the old spot; the gate swings differently, new thatch has been put on the old gables, the road has been widened, and the sward the driven sheep lingered on is gone. Who dares to think then? For faces fade as flowers, and there is no consolation. So now I am sure I was right in always walking the same way by the starry flowers striving upwards on a slender ancestry of stem; I would follow the plain old road to-day if I could. Let change be far from me; that irresistible change must come is bitter indeed. Give me the old road, the same flowers — they were only stitchwort — the old succession of days and garland, ever weaving into it fresh wild flowers from far and near. Fetch them from distant mountains, discover them on decaying walls, in unsuspected corners; though never seen before, still they are the same: there has been a place in the heart waiting for them.

The Sun and the Brook

THE sun first sees the brook in the meadow where some roach swim under a bulging root of ash. Leaning against the tree, and looking down into the water, there is a picture of the sky. Its brightness hides the sandy floor of the stream as a picture conceals the wall where it hangs, but, as if the water cooled the rays, the eye can bear to gaze on the image of the sun. Over its circle thin threads of summer cloud are drawn; it is only the reflection, yet the sun seems closer seen in the brook, more to do with us, like the grass, and the tree, and the flowing stream. In the sky it is so far, it cannot be approached, nor even gazed at, so that by the very virtue and power of its own brilliance it forces us to ignore, and almost forget it. The summer days go on, and no one notices the sun. The sweet water slipping past the green flags, with every now and then a rushing sound of eager haste, receives the sky, and it becomes a part of the earth and of life. No one can see his own face without a glass; no one can sit down and deliberately think of the soul till it appears a visible thing. It eludes — the mind cannot grasp it. But hold a flower in the hand — a rose, this later honeysuckle, or this the first harebell — and in its beauty you can recognize your own soul reflected as the sun in the brook. For the soul finds itself in beautiful things.

Between the bulging root and the bank there is a tiny oval pool, on the surface of which the light does not fall. There the eye can see deep down into the stream, which scarcely moves in the hollow it has worn for itself as its weight swings into the concave of the bend. The hollow is illuminated by the light which sinks through the stream outside the root; and beneath, in the green depth, five or six roach face the current. Every now and then a tiny curl appears on the surface inside the root, and must rise up to come there. Unwinding as it goes, its raised edge lowers and becomes lost in the level. Dark moss on the base of the ash darkens the water under. The light green leaves overhead yield gently to the passing air; there are but few leaves on the tree, and these scarcely make a shadow on the grass beyond that of the trunk. As the branch swings, the gnats are driven farther away to avoid it. Over the verge of the bank, bending down almost to the root in the water, droop the heavily seeded heads of tall grasses which, growing there, have escaped the scythe.

These are the days of the convolvulus, of ripening berry, and dropping nut. In the gateways, ears of wheat hang from the hawthorn boughs, which seized them from the passing load. The broad aftermath is without flowers; the flowers are gone to the uplands and the untilled wastes. Curving opposite the south, the hollow side of the brook has received the sunlight like a silvered speculum every day that the sun has shone. Since the first violet of the meadow, till now that the berries are ripening, through all the long drama of the summer, the rays have visited the stream. The long, loving touch of the sun has left some of its own mystic attraction in the brook. Resting here, and gazing down into it, thoughts and dreams come flowing as the water flows. Thoughts without words, mobile like the stream, nothing compact that can be grasped and stayed: dreams that slip silently as water slips through the fingers. The grass is not grass alone; the leaves of the ash above are not leaves only. From tree, and earth, and soft air moving, there comes an invisible touch which arranges the senses to its waves as the ripples of the lake set the sand in parallel lines. The grass sways and fans the reposing mind; the leaves sway and stroke it, till it can feel beyond itself and with them, using each grass blade, each leaf, to abstract life from earth and ether. These then become new organs, fresh nerves and veins running afar out into the field, along the winding brook, up through the leaves, bringing a larger existence. The arms of the mind open wide to the broad sky.

Some sense of the meaning of the grass, and leaves of the tree, and sweet waters hovers on the confines of thought, and seems ready to be resolved into definite form. There is a meaning in these things, a meaning in all that exists, and it comes near to declare itself. Not yet, not fully, nor in such shape that it may be formulated — if ever it will be — but sufficiently so to leave, as it were, an unwritten impression that will remain when the glamour is gone, and grass is but grass, and a tree a tree.

The July Grass

A JULY fly went sideways over the long grass. His wings made a burr about him like a net, beating so fast they wrapped him round with a cloud. Every now and then, as he flew over the trees of grass, a taller one than common stopped him, and there he clung, and then the eye had time to see the scarlet spots — the loveliest colour — on his wings. The wind swung the burnet and loosened his hold, and away he went again over the grasses, and not one jot did he care if they were *Poa* or *Festuca*, or *Bromus* or *Hordeum*, or any other name. Names were nothing to him; all he had to do was to whirl his scarlet spots about in the brilliant sun, rest when he liked, and go on again. I wonder whether it is a joy to have bright scarlet spots, and to be clad in the purple and gold of life; is the colour felt by the creature that wears it? The rose, restful of a dewy morn before the sunbeams have topped the garden wall, must feel a joy in its own fragrance, and know the exquisite hue of its stained petals. The rose sleeps in its beauty.

The fly whirls his scarlet-spotted wings about and splashes himself with sunlight, like the children on the sands. He thinks not of the grass and sun; he does not heed them at all — and that is why he is so happy — any more than the barefoot children ask why the sea is there, or why it does not quite dry up when it ebbs. He is unconscious; he lives without thinking about living; and if the sunshine were a hundred hours long, still it would not be long enough. No, never enough of sun and sliding shadows that come like a hand over the table to lovingly reach our shoulder, never enough of the grass that smells sweet as a flower, not if we could live years and years equal in number to the tides that have ebbed and flowed counting backwards for years to every day and night, backwards till we found out which came first, the night or the day. The scarlet-dotted fly knows nothing of the names of the grasses that grow here where the sward nears the sea, and thinking of him I have decided not to wilfully seek to learn any more of their names either. My big grass book I have left at home, and the dust is settling on the gold of the binding. I have picked a handful this morning of which I know nothing. I will sit here on the turf and the scarlet-dotted flies shall pass over me, as if I too were but a grass. I will not think, I will be unconscious, I will live.

A SHORT BIBLIOGRAPHY

BOOKS BY RICHARD JEFFERIES

1874 *The Scarlet Shawl: a novel.* London: Tinsley.

1875 *Restless Human Hearts: a novel.* 3 vols. London: Tinsley.

1877 *World's End: A Story in Three Books.* 3. vols. London: Tinsley.

1878 *The Gamekeeper at Home; or, Sketches of Natural History and Rural Life.* London: Smith, Elder.
STILL IN PRINT with The Amateur Poacher in one volume. O.U.P. paperback.

1879 *Wildlife in a Southern County.* London: Smith, Elder.

1879 *The Amateur Poacher.* London: Smith, Elder.
STILL IN PRINT with The Gamekeeper at Home in one volume. O.U.P. paperback.

1880 *Greene Ferne Farm.* London: Smith, Elder.

1880 *Hodge and His Masters.* 2 vols. London: Smith, Elder.
STILL IN PRINT in one volume. Quartet Books paperback.

1880 *Round About a Great Estate.* London: Smith, Elder.

1881 *Wood Magic:* a fable. 2 vols. London: Cassell.

1882 *Bevis: The Story of a Boy.* 3 vols. London: Sampson Low.
STILL IN PRINT in one volume. Everyman Paperbacks (Dent).

1883 *Nature Near London*. London: Chatto & Windus. Contents: Woodlands, Footpaths, Flocks of Birds, Nightingale Road, A Brook, A London Trout, A Barn, Wheatfields, The Crows, Heathlands, The River, Nutty Autumn, Round a London Copse, Magpie Fields, Herbs, Trees About Town, To Brighton, The Southdown Shepherd, The Breeze on Beachy Head.
STILL IN PRINT. John Clare Books.

1883 *The Story of My Heart: My Autobiography*. London: Longmans, Green.
STILL IN PRINT. Quartet Books paperback.

1884 *Red Deer*. London: Longmans, Green.

1884 *The Life of the Fields*. London: Chatto & Windus. Contents: The Field-Play, Bits of Oak Bark, The Pageant of Summer, Meadow Thoughts, Clematis Lane, Nature Near Brighton, Sea Sky and Down, January in the Sussex Woods, By the Axe, The Water-Colley, Notes on Landscape Painting, Village Miners, Mind Under Water, Sport and Science, Nature and the Gamekeeper, The Sacrifice to Trout, The Hovering of the Kestrel, Birds Climbing the Air, Country Literature, Sunlight in a London Square, Venice in the East End, The Pigeons at The British Museum, The Plainest City in Europe.

1884 *The Dewy Morn: a novel*. 2 vols. London: Bentley.
STILL IN PRINT. Wildwood House, paperback.

1885 *After London; or, Wild England*. London: Cassell.
STILL IN PRINT. O.U.P., paperback.

1885 *The Open Air*. London: Chatto & Windus.
Contents: Saint Guido, Golden-Brown, Wild Flowers, Sunny Brighton, The Pine Wood, Nature on the Roof, One of the New Voters, The Modern Thames, The Single-Barrel Gun, The Haunt of the Hare, The Bathing Season, Under the Acorns, Downs, Forest, Beauty in the Country, Out of Doors in February, Haunts of the Lapwing, Outside London, On the London Road, Red Roofs of London, A Wet Night in London.
STILL IN PRINT. Wildwood House, paperback.

1887 *Amaryllis at the Fair*. London: Sampson Low.
STILL IN PRINT. Quartet Books, paperback.

1889 *Field and Hedgerow: Being the Last Essays of Richard Jefferies, Collected by His Widow*. London: Longmans, Green.
Contents: Hours of Spring, Nature and Books, The July Grass, Winds of Heaven, The Country Sunday, The Country-side, Sussex, Swallow-Time, Buckhurst Park, House-Martins, Among the Nuts, Walks in the Wheatfields, Just Before Winter, Locality and Nature, Country Places, Field Words and Ways, Cottage Ideas, April Gossip, Some April Insects, The Time of Year, Mixed Days of May and December, The Makers of Summer, Steam on Country Roads, Field Sports in Art, Birds' Nests, Nature in the Louvre, Summer in Somerset, An English Deer-park, My Old Village, My Chaffinch (poem).

1892 *The Toilers of the Field*. London: Longmans, Green.
Contents: Part I — The Farmer at Home, The Labourers' Daily Life, Field-faring Women, An

English Homestead, John Smith's Shanty, Wiltshire Labourers *(Letters to The Times)*, A True Tale of the Wiltshire Labourer. Part II — the Coming of Summer, the Golden-crested Wren, An Extinct Race, *Orchis Mascula*, The Lions in Trafalgar Square.
STILL IN PRINT. Heritage (Futura Paperbacks)

1909 *The Hills and the Vale.* London: Duckworth. Contents: Choosing a Gun, Skating, Marlborough Forest, Village Churches, Birds of Spring, The Spring of the Year, Vignettes from Nature (Spring, The Green Corn), A King of Acres, The Story of Swindon, Unequal Agriculture, Village Organisation, the Idle Earth, After the County Franchise, The Wiltshire Labourer, On the Downs, The Sun and the Brook, Nature and Eternity, The Dawn.
STILL IN PRINT. O.U.P., paperback.

1948 *The Old House at Coate and Other Hitherto Unpublished Essays by Richard Jefferies.* Collected by Samuel J. Looker. London: Lutterworth Press. Contents: The Blue Doors, The Seasons and the Stars, Birds and People, Under the Apple Tree, Life Force, Flying Machines, The Buttercups, From the Tree to the Pool, Absence of Design in Nature, The Prodigality of Nature and Niggardliness of Man, Aerial Navigation and the Flight of Birds and Insects, The Wall below the Apple Tree, The Seasons in Surrey: Tree and Bird Life in the Copse, The Last of a London Trout, Trees in and around London, Three Centuries at Home, Strength of the English, The Squire and the Land, The Life of the Soul.

1948 *The Nature Diaries and Note-Books of Richard Jefferies.* Edited by Samuel J. Looker. London: Grey Walls Press.

1979 *The Pageant of Summer.* Essays selected by Andrew Rossabi. London: Quartet Books, paperback. *STILL IN PRINT.*

BIOGRAPHY

1909 *Richard Jefferies, His Life and Work,* by Edward Thomas. London: Hutchinson. *STILL IN PRINT.* Faber Paperbacks.

1964 *Richard Jefferies, Man of the Fields,* by Samuel J. Looker and Crichton Porteous. London: John Baker. *Out of Print, but well worth looking for.*

There are other volumes of essays compiled and edited by the late Samuel J. Looker. Students of Jefferies will long have reason to be grateful to Mr Looker. During his lifetime, with understanding and dedication to his subject, he did more to keep Jefferies' work to the fore than anyone else in recent years.